OTTO'S
BACKWARDS DAY

FRANK CAMMUSO

with **JAY LYNCH**

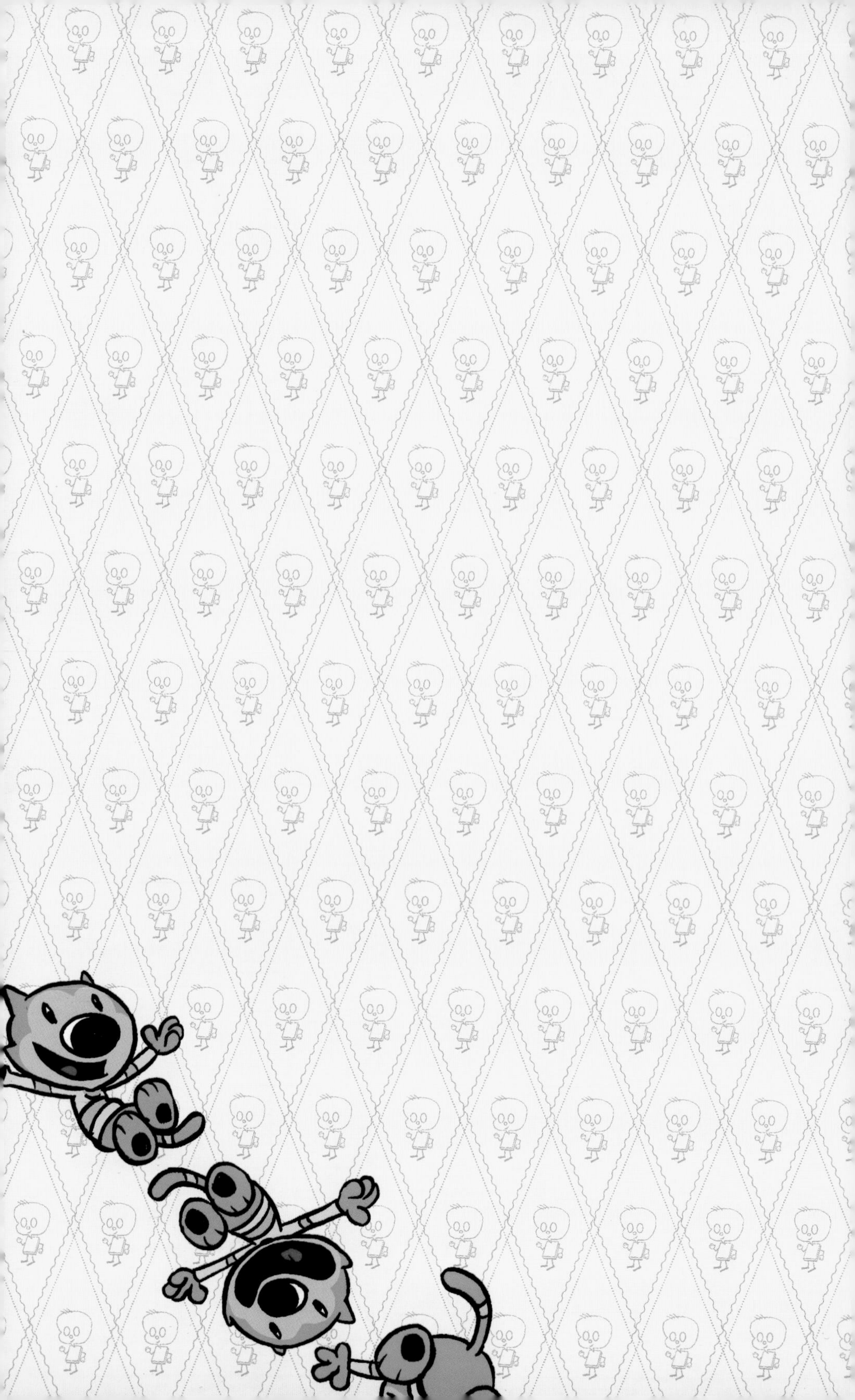

OTTO'S
BACKWARDS DAY

A TOON BOOK BY

FRANK CAMMUSO
with JAY LYNCH

ABDO Spotlight

For Khai

Editorial Director: **FRANÇOISE MOULY** · Book Design: **FRANÇOISE MOULY & JONATHAN BENNETT**

FRANK CAMMUSO'S artwork was drawn in india ink and colored digitally.

ABDOPUBLISHING.COM

Reinforced library bound edition published in 2016 by Spotlight, a division of ABDO
PO Box 398166, Minneapolis, Minnesota 55439. Spotlight produces high-quality reinforced library bound
editions for schools and libraries. Published by agreement with TOON Books.

Printed in the United States of America, North Mankato, Minnesota.
092015
012016

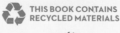

**THIS BOOK CONTAINS
RECYCLED MATERIALS**

A
TOON
BOOK

WWW.TOON-BOOKS.COM

LIBRARY OF CONGRESS CATALOGING-IN-PUBLICATION DATA

This book was previously cataloged with the following information:

Cammuso, Frank, author, illustrator.
 Otto's backwards day : a TOON book / by Frank Cammuso with Jay Lynch.
  pages cm. -- (Easy-to-read comics. Level 3)
Summary: "Someone stole Otto's birthday! When Otto the cat and his robot sidekick Toot follow the crook,
they discover a topsy-turvy world where rats chase cats and people wear underpants over their clothes"--
Provided by publisher.
ISBN 978-1-935179-33-7 (alk. paper)
1. Graphic novels. [1. Graphic novels. 2. Birthdays--Fiction. 3. Cats--Fiction. 4. Humorous stories.] I. Lynch,
Jay, author. II. Title.
PZ7.7.C36Or 2013
741.5'973--dc23

                2012047661

ISBN 978-1-61479-426-4 (reinforced library bound edition)

Spotlight

A Division of ABDO
abdopublishing.com

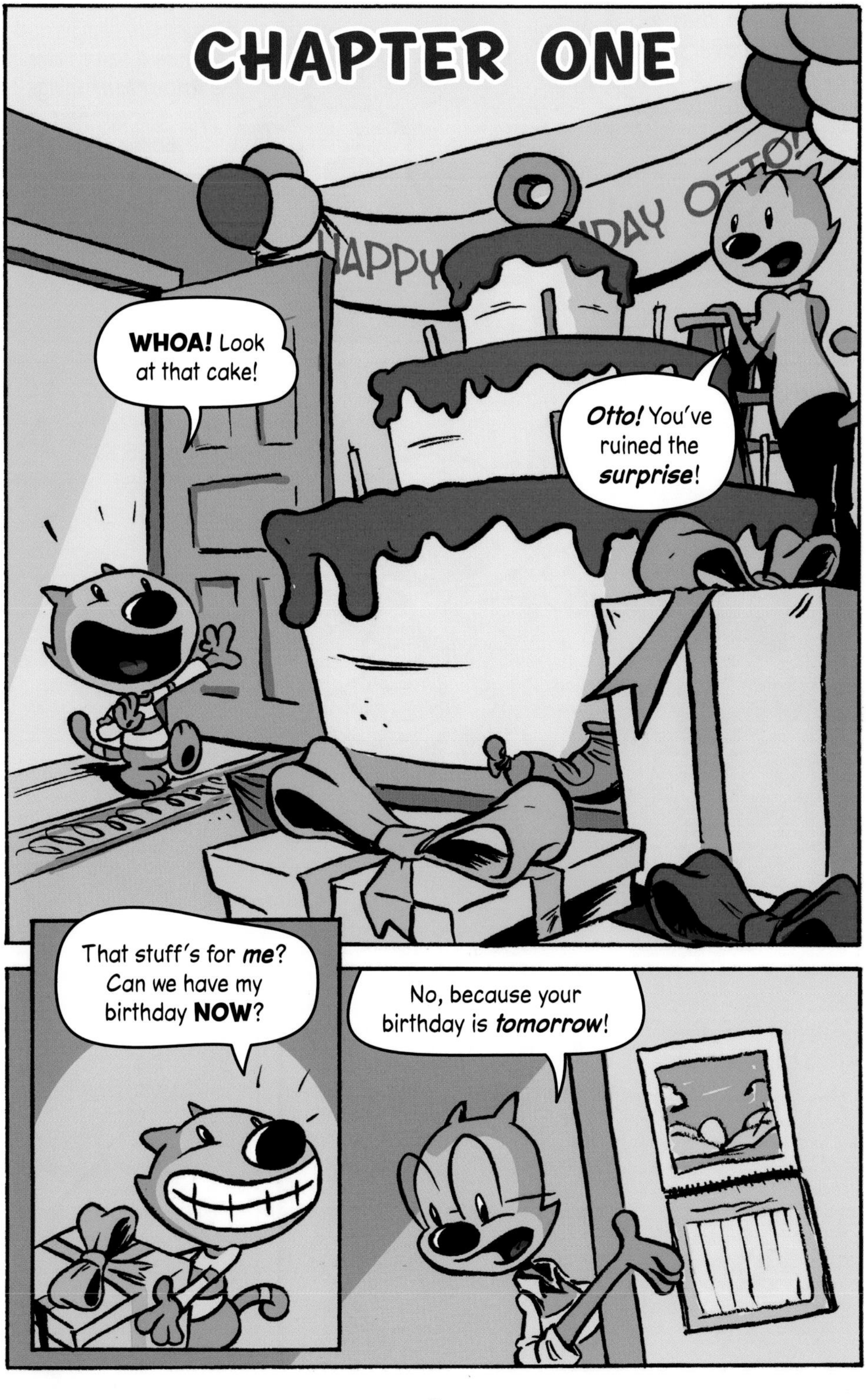
CHAPTER ONE
HAPPY ...DAY OTTO!
WHOA! Look at that cake!
Otto! You've ruined the surprise!
That stuff's for me? Can we have my birthday NOW?
No, because your birthday is tomorrow!

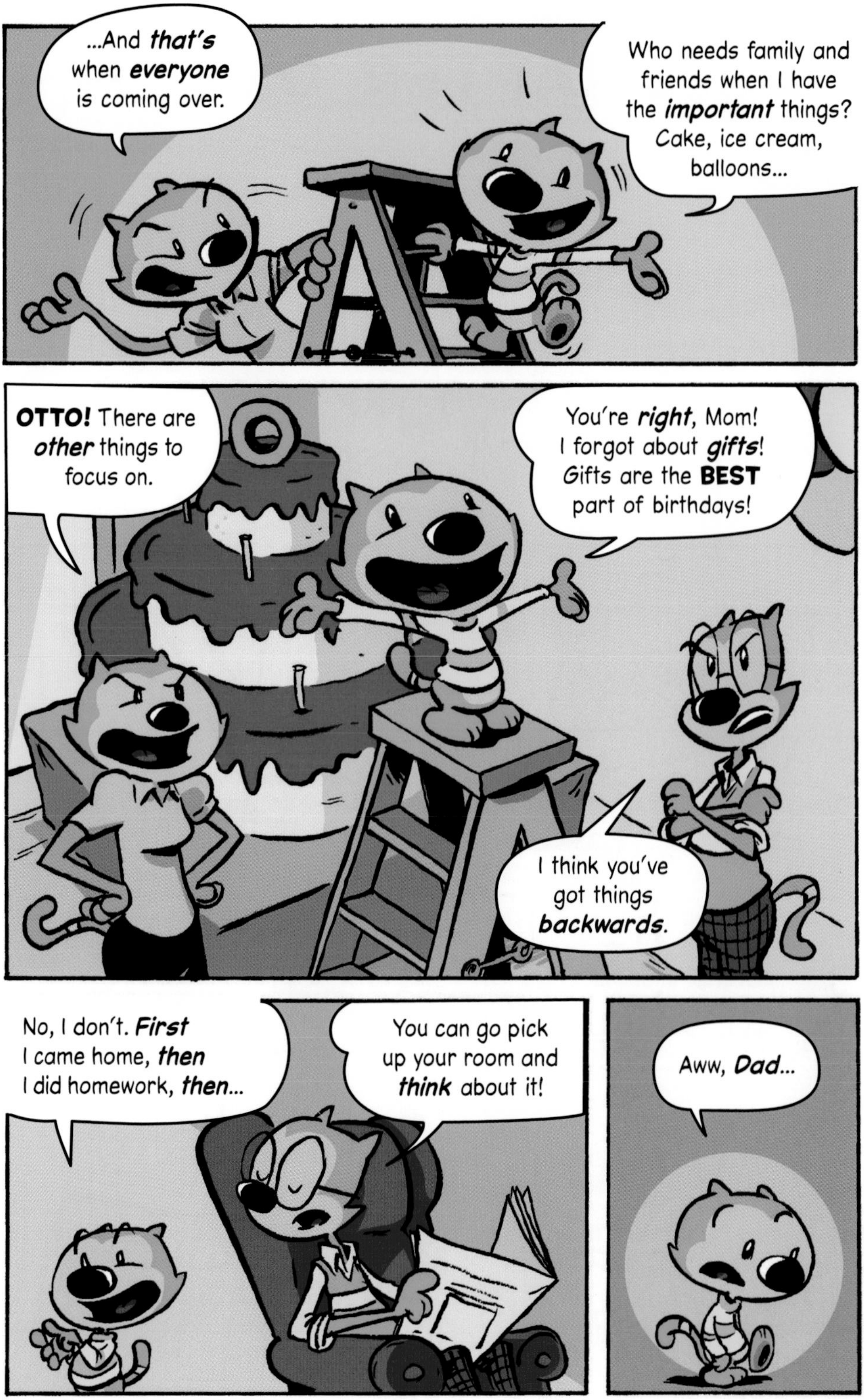
...And *that's* when *everyone* is coming over.
Who needs family and friends when I have the *important* things? Cake, ice cream, balloons...
OTTO! There are *other* things to focus on.
You're *right*, Mom! I forgot about *gifts*! Gifts are the **BEST** part of birthdays!
I think you've got things *backwards*.
No, I don't. *First* I came home, *then* I did homework, *then*...
You can go pick up your room and *think* about it!
Aww, *Dad*...

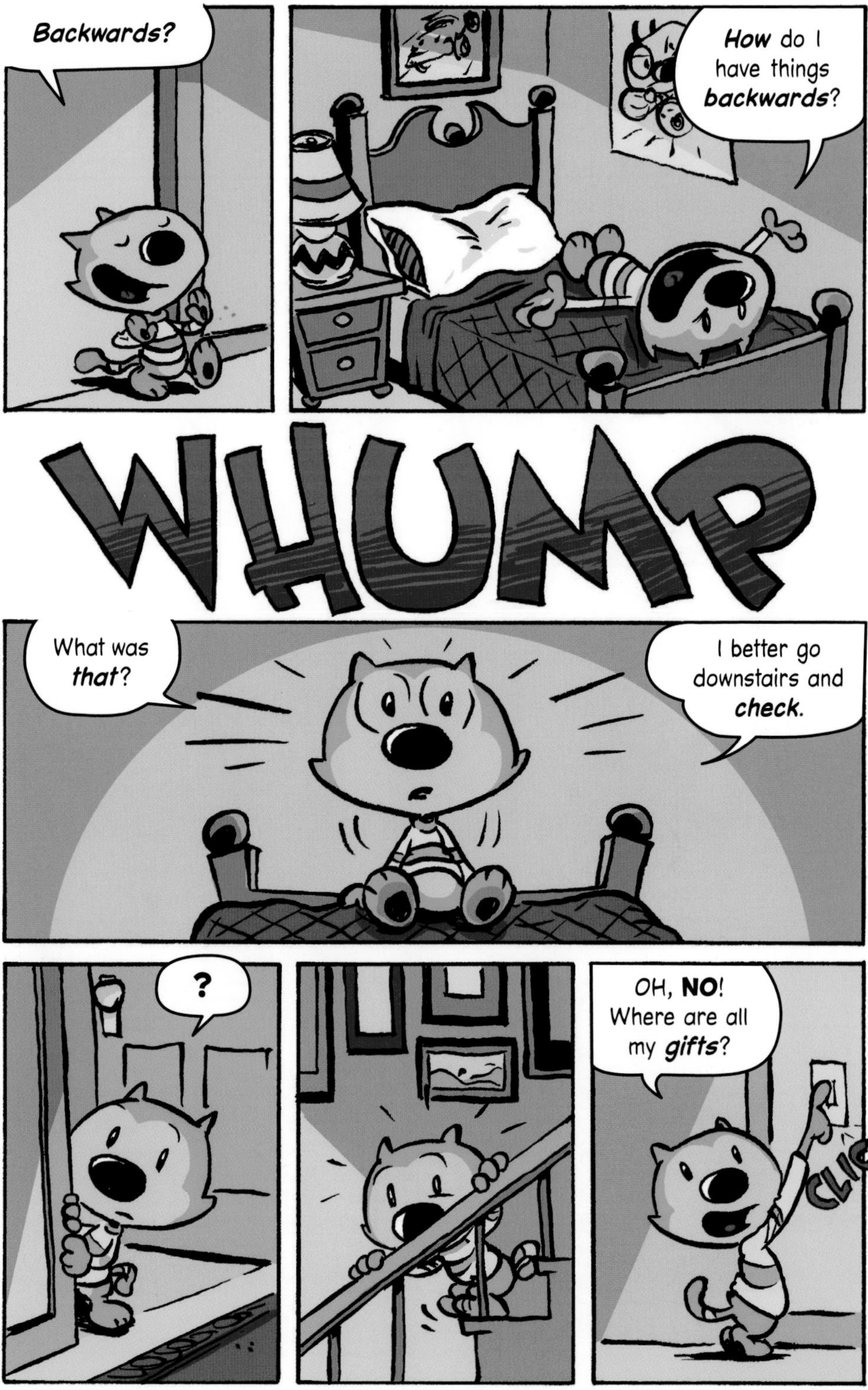
Backwards?
How do I have things backwards?
WHUMP
What was that?
I better go downstairs and check.
?
OH, NO! Where are all my gifts?
CLICK

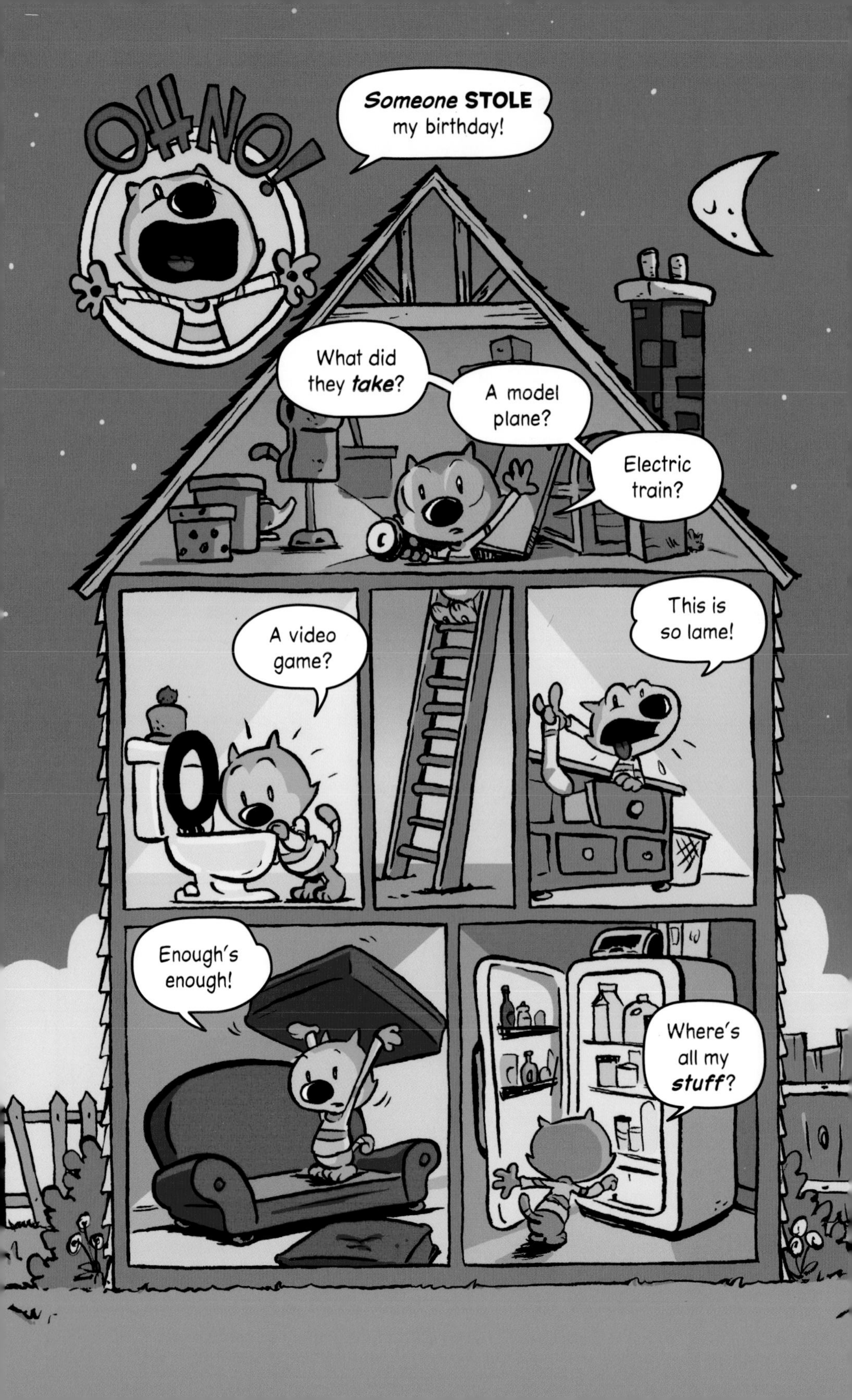
OH NO!
Someone STOLE my birthday!
What did they take?
A model plane?
Electric train?
A video game?
This is so lame!
Enough's enough!
Where's all my stuff?

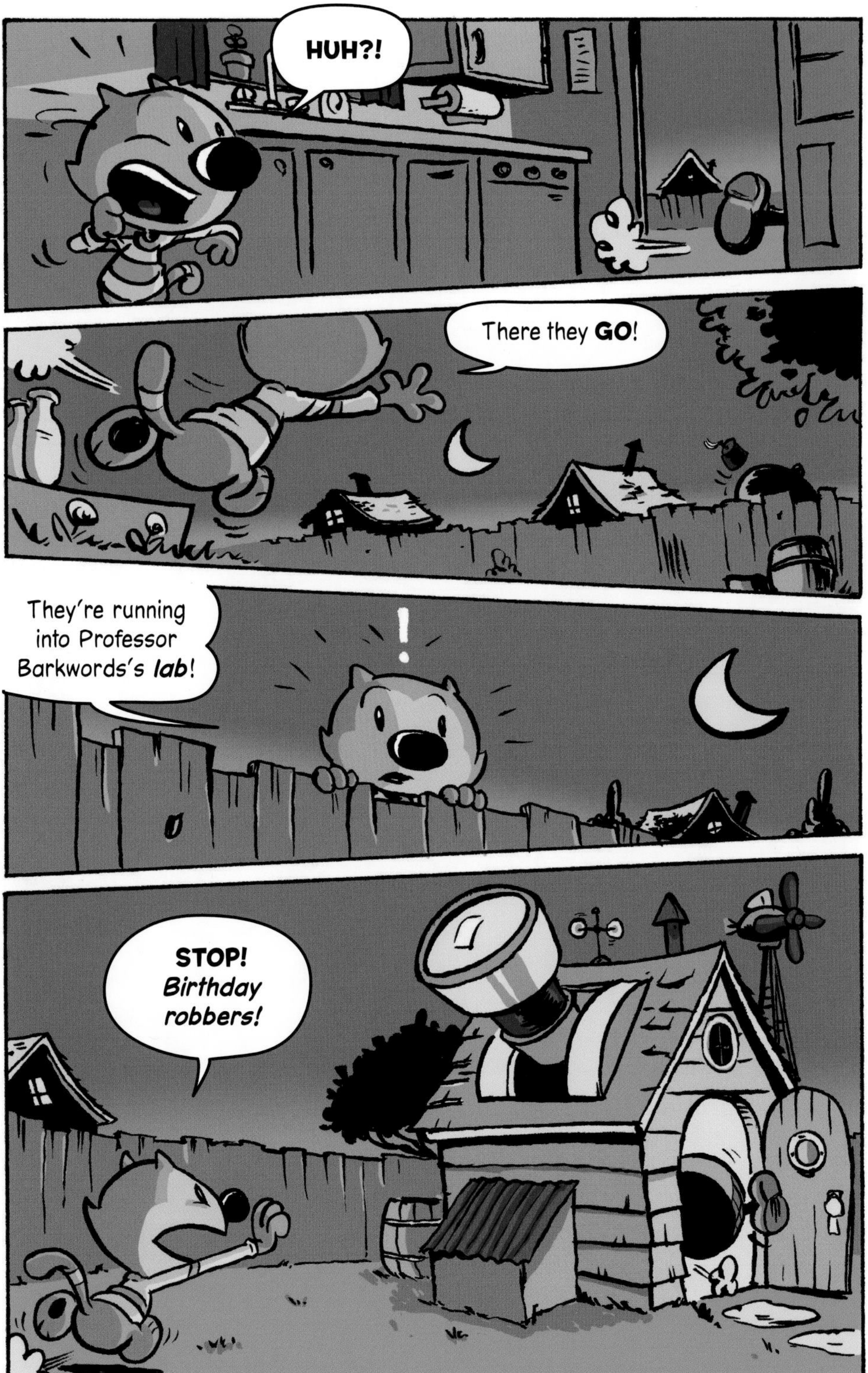
HUH?!
There they **GO**!
They're running into Professor Barkwords's *lab*!
STOP! *Birthday robbers!*

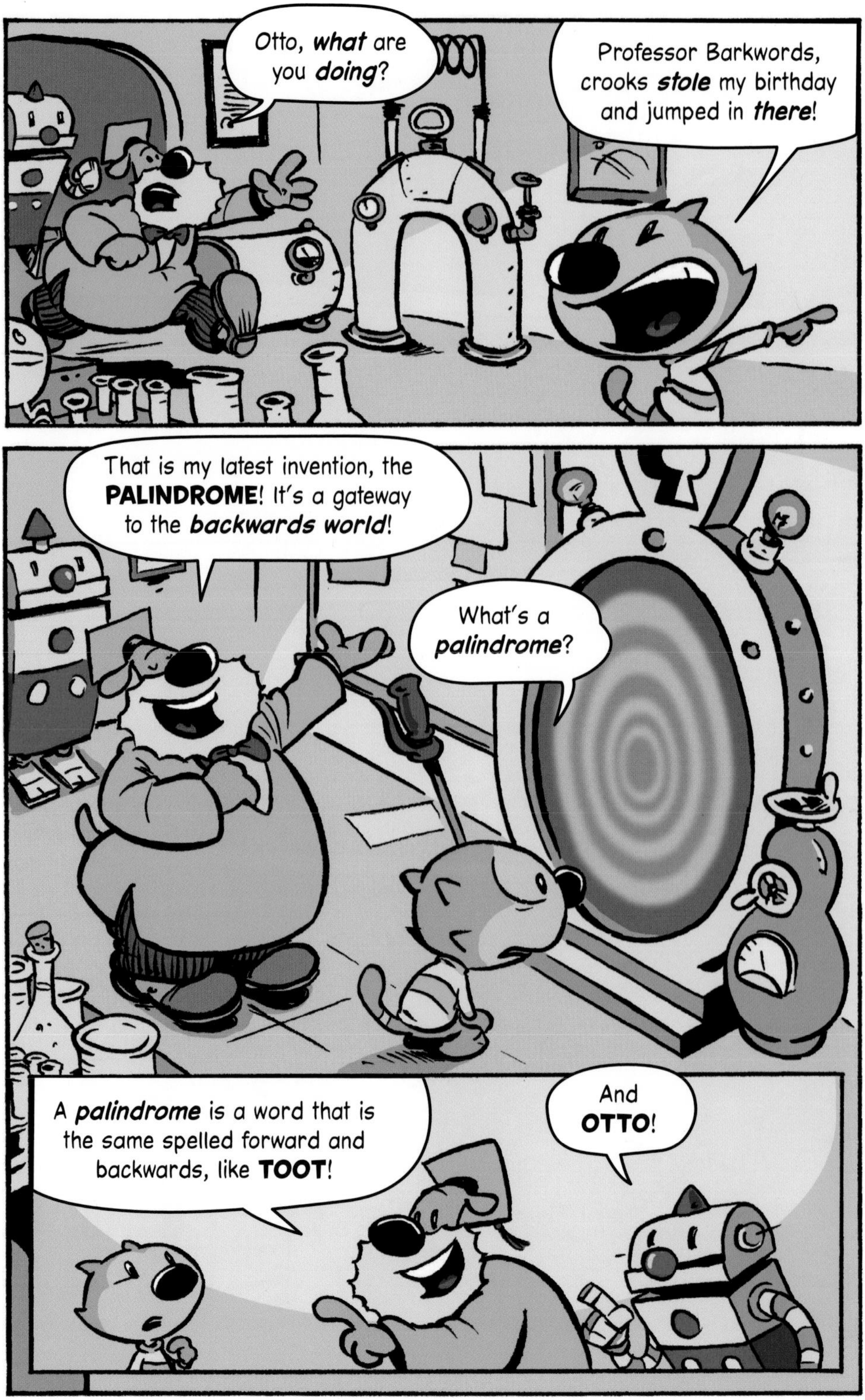
Otto, *what* are you *doing*?
Professor Barkwords, crooks *stole* my birthday and jumped in *there*!
That is my latest invention, the **PALINDROME**! It's a gateway to the *backwards world*!
What's a *palindrome*?
A *palindrome* is a word that is the same spelled forward and backwards, like **TOOT**!
And **OTTO**!

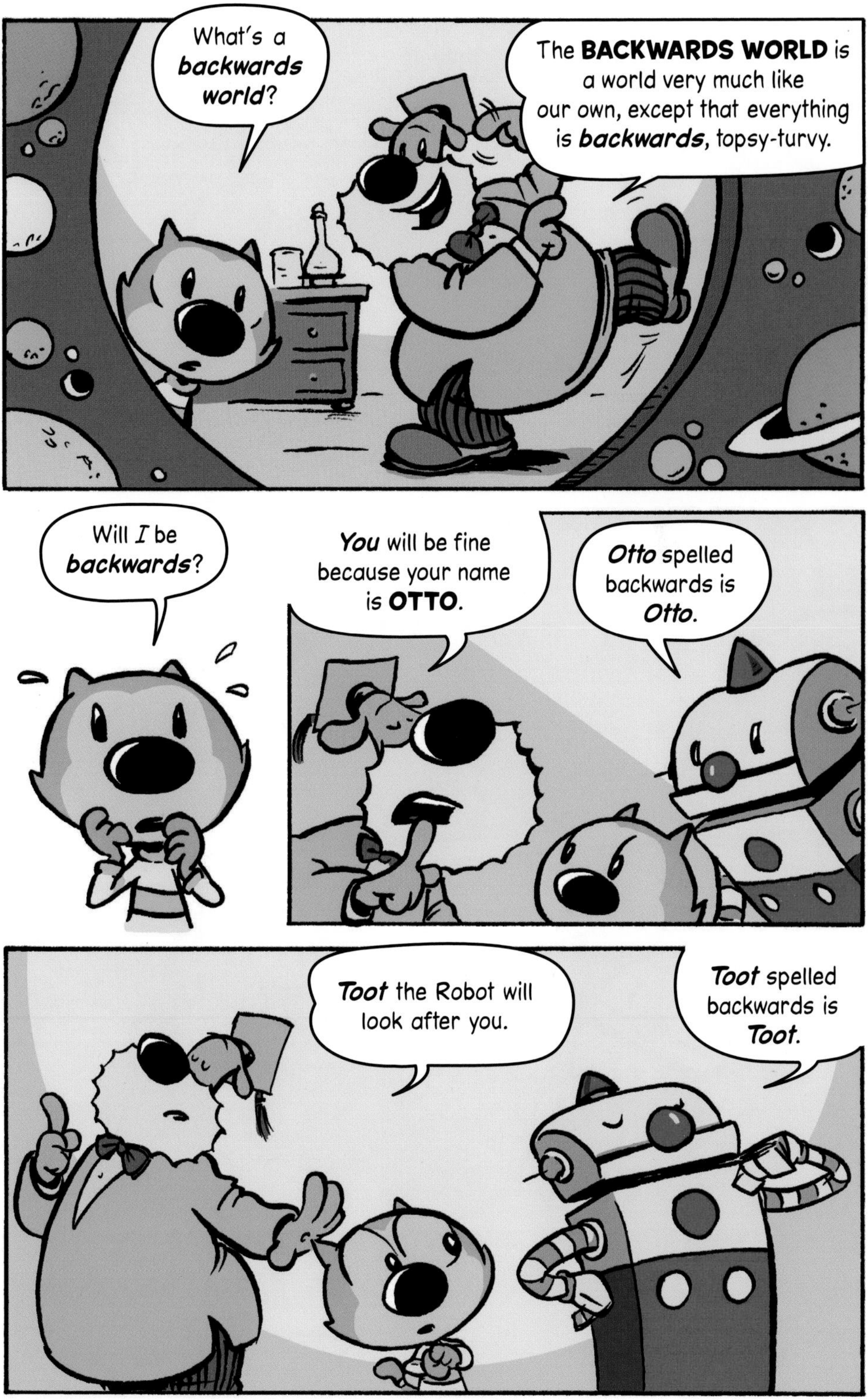
What's a *backwards world*?
The **BACKWARDS WORLD** is a world very much like our own, except that everything is ***backwards,*** topsy-turvy.
Will *I* be ***backwards***?
You will be fine because your name is **OTTO**.
Otto spelled backwards is ***Otto***.
Toot the Robot will look after you.
Toot spelled backwards is ***Toot***.

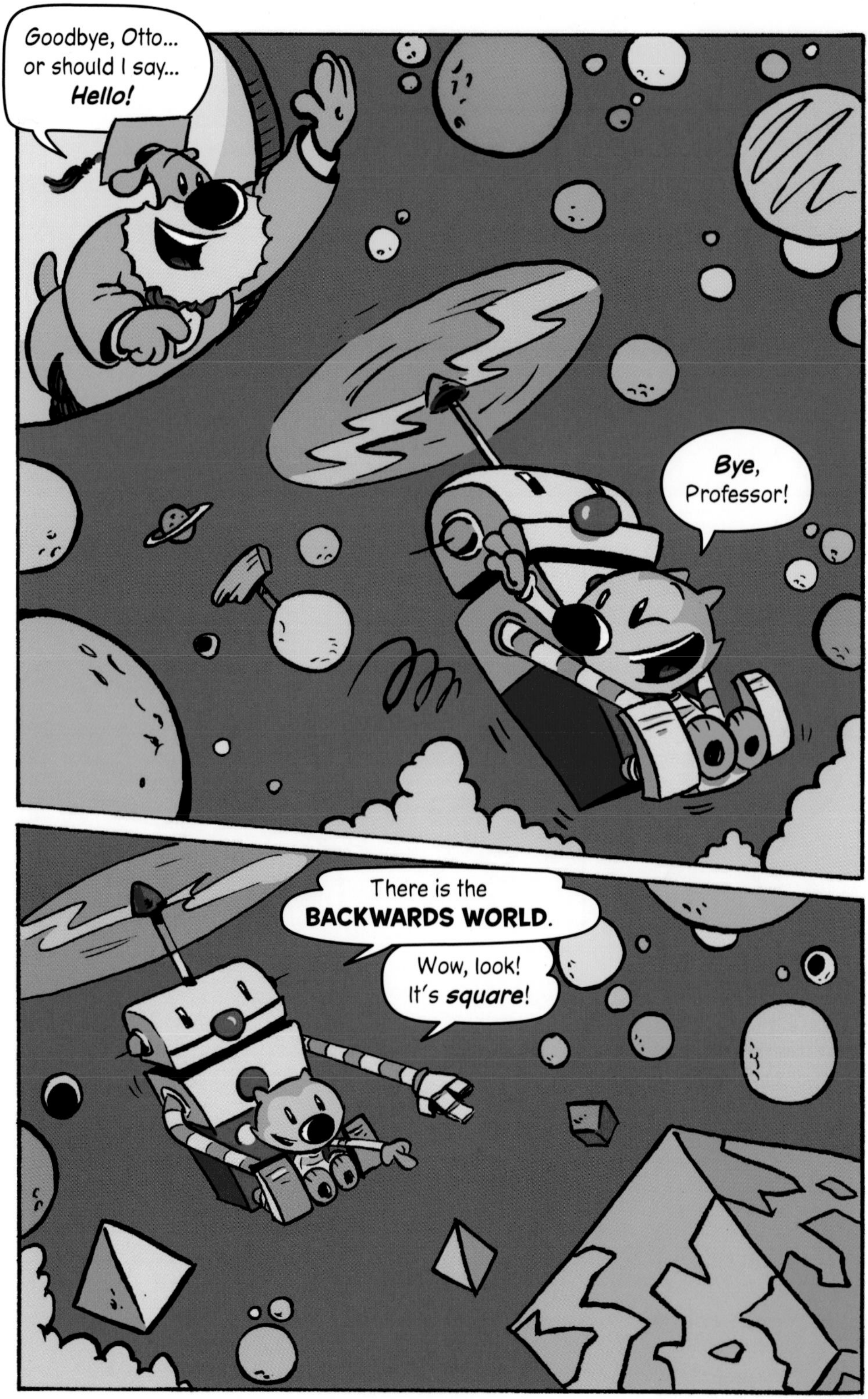
Goodbye, Otto... or should I say... **Hello!**
Bye, Professor!
There is the **BACKWARDS WORLD**.
Wow, look! It's ***square***!

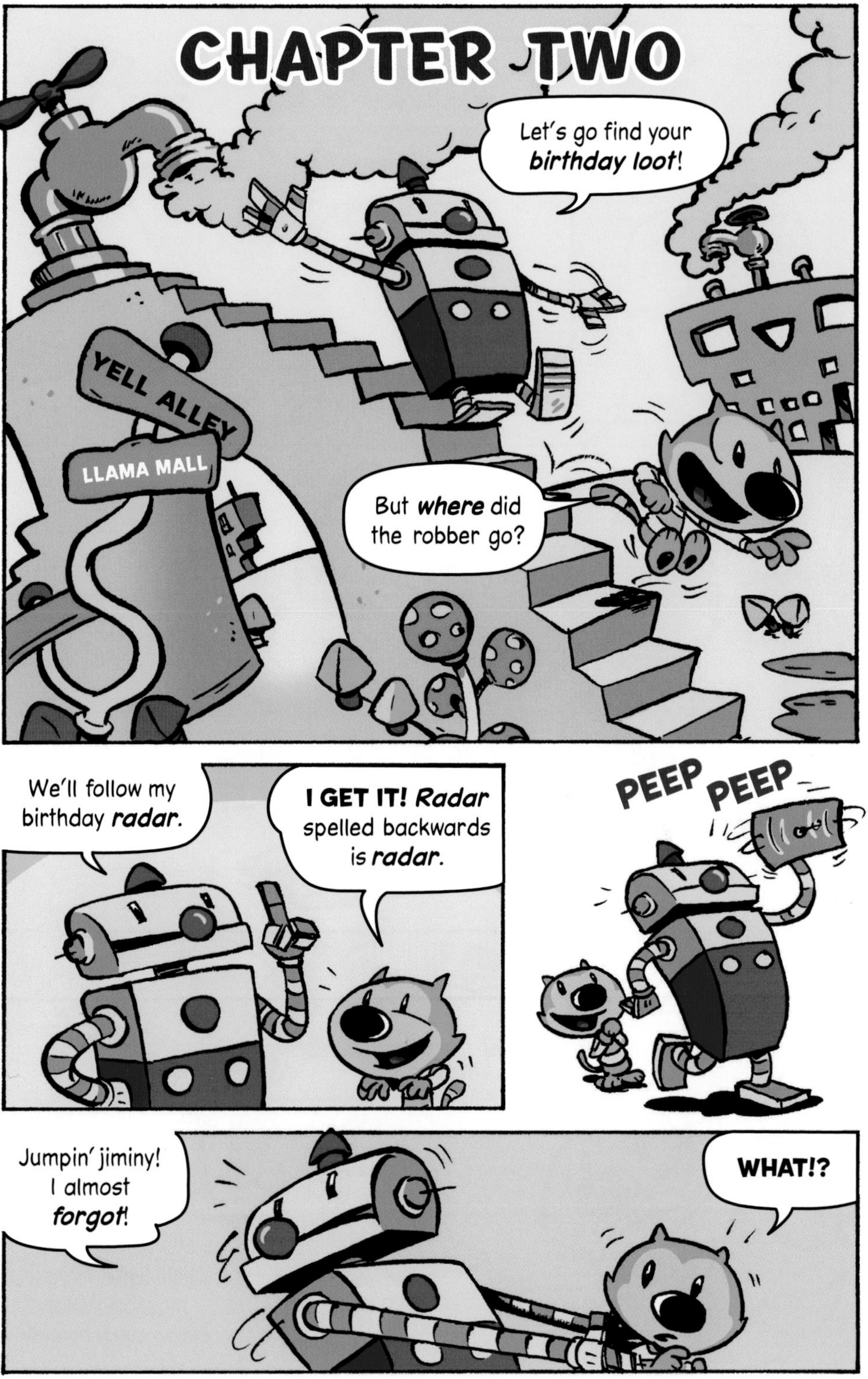
CHAPTER TWO
Let's go find your *birthday loot*!
YELL ALLEY
LLAMA MALL
But *where* did the robber go?
We'll follow my birthday *radar*.
I GET IT! *Radar* spelled backwards is *radar*.
PEEP PEEP
Jumpin' jiminy! I almost *forgot*!
WHAT!?

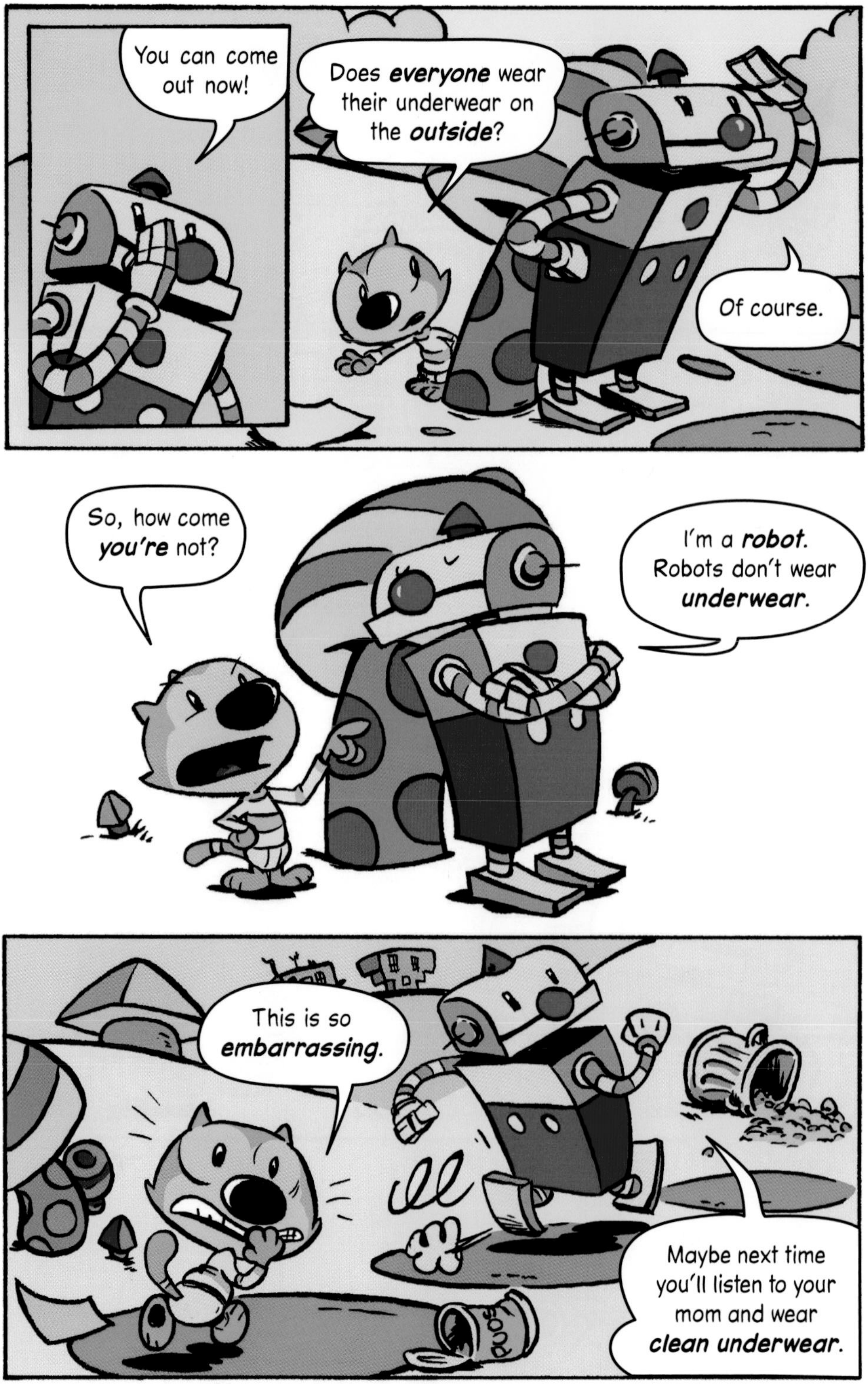
You can come out now!
Does everyone wear their underwear on the outside?
Of course.
So, how come you're not?
I'm a robot. Robots don't wear underwear.
This is so embarrassing.
Maybe next time you'll listen to your mom and wear clean underwear.

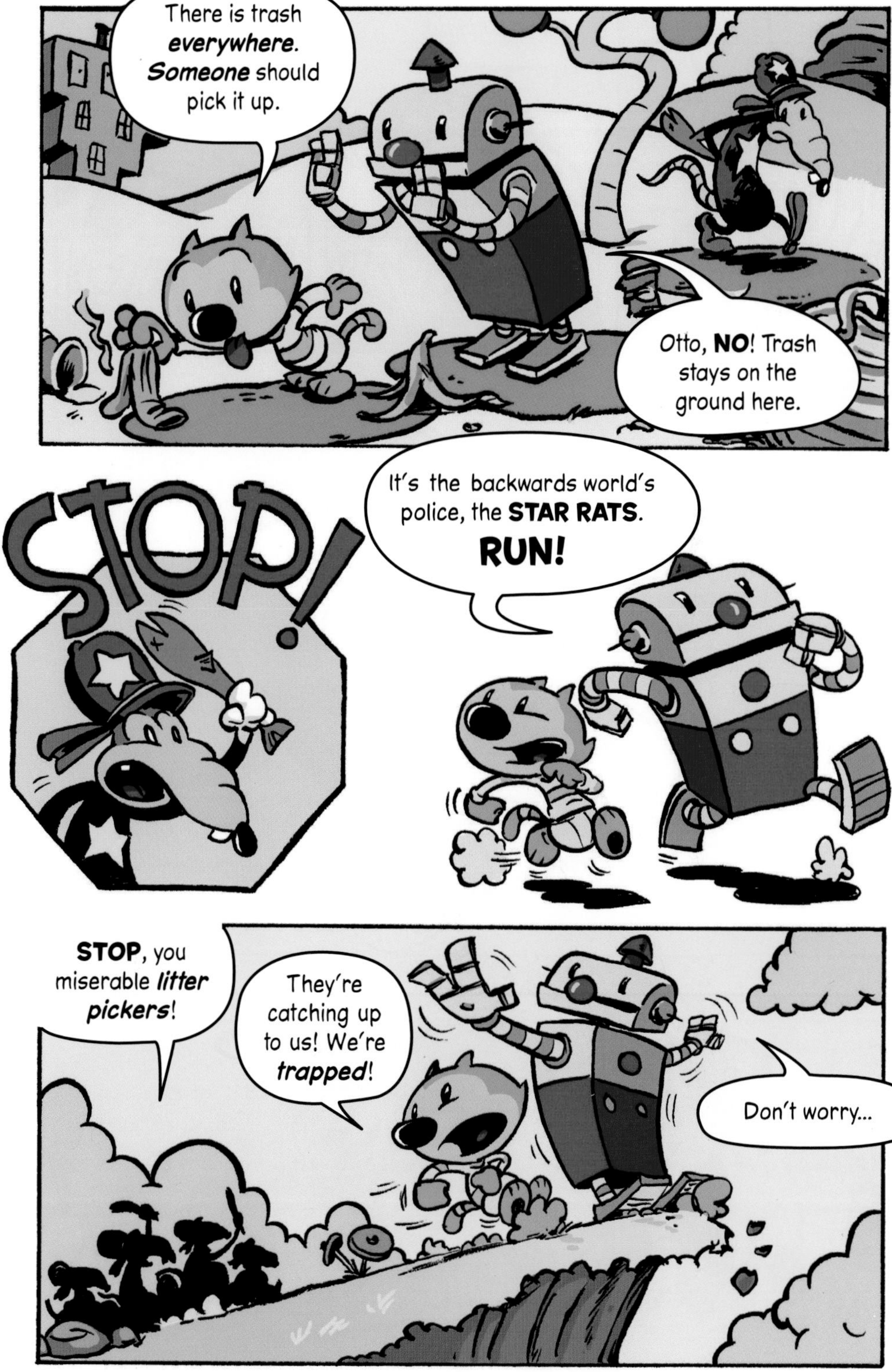
There is trash *everywhere*. *Someone* should pick it up.
Otto, **NO**! Trash stays on the ground here.
STOP!
It's the backwards world's police, the **STAR RATS**. **RUN!**
STOP, you miserable *litter pickers*!
They're catching up to us! We're *trapped*!
Don't worry...

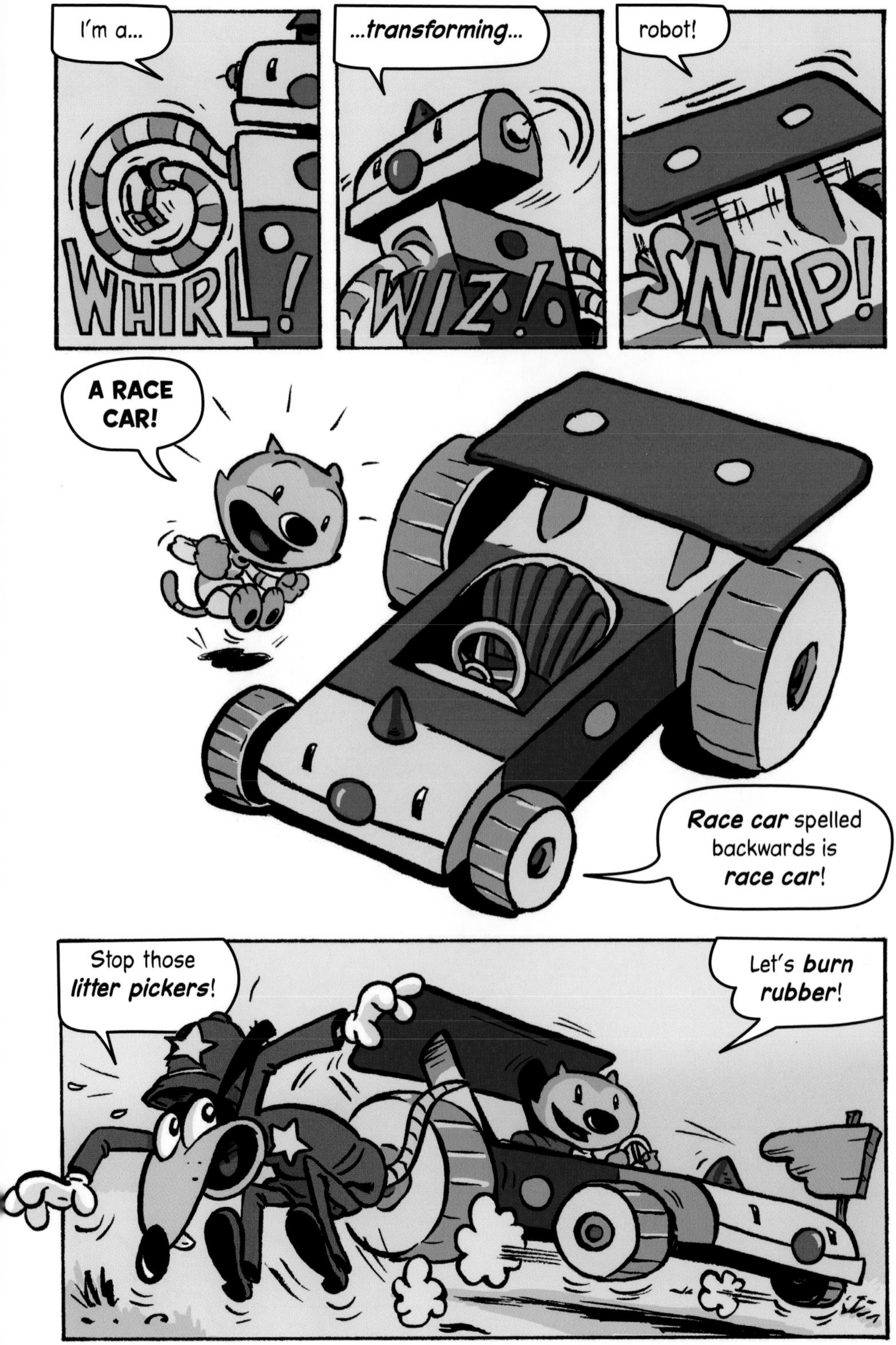
I'm a...
WHIRL!
...transforming...
WIZ!
robot!
SNAP!
A RACE CAR!
Race car spelled backwards is race car!
Stop those litter pickers!
Let's burn rubber!

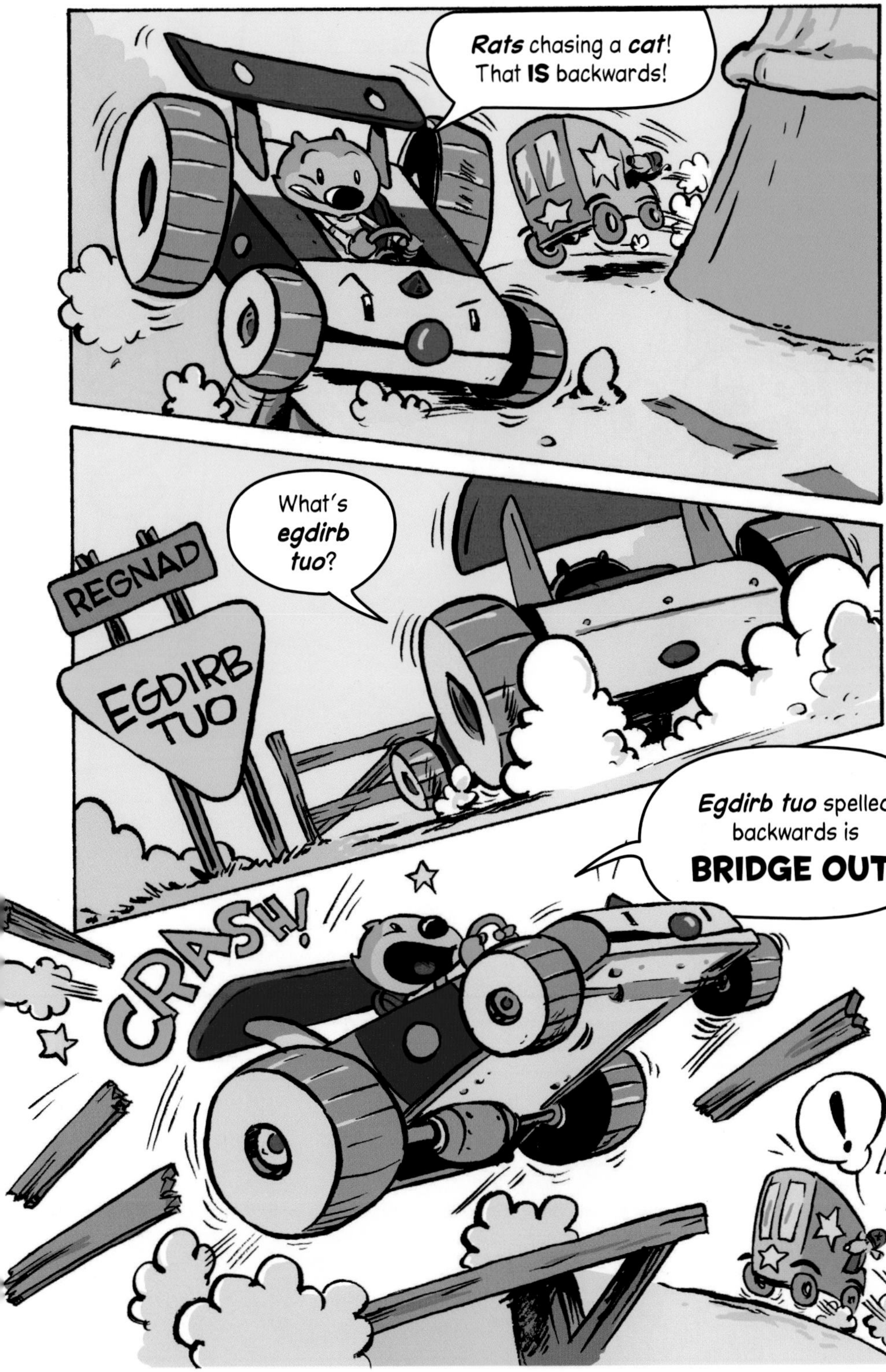
Rats chasing a *cat*! That **IS** backwards!
What's *egdirb tuo*?
REGNAD
EGDIRB TUO
Egdirb tuo spelled backwards is **BRIDGE OUT**!
CRASH!
!

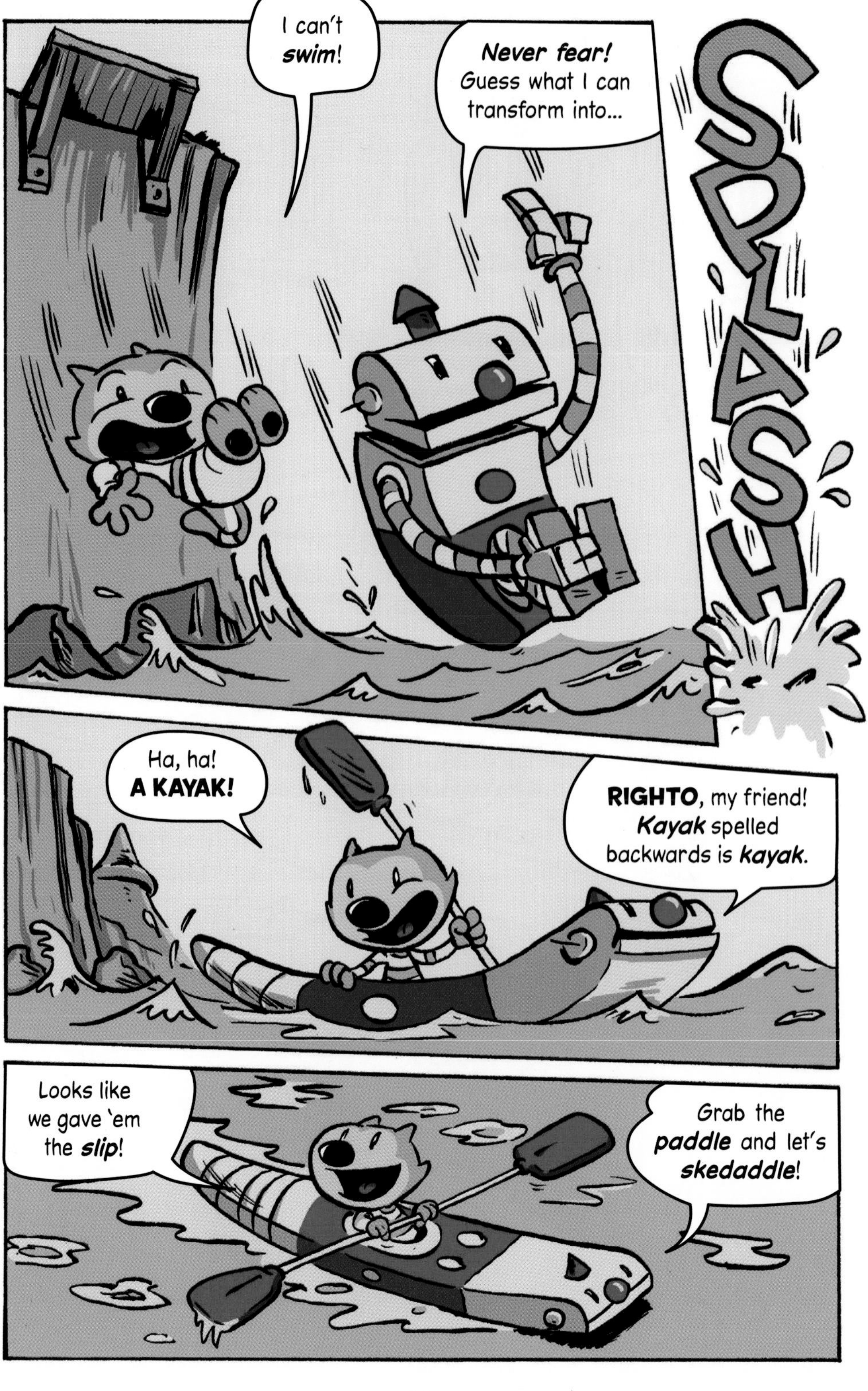
I can't **swim**!
Never fear! Guess what I can transform into...
SPLASH
Ha, ha! **A KAYAK!**
RIGHTO, my friend! ***Kayak*** spelled backwards is ***kayak***.
Looks like we gave 'em the ***slip***!
Grab the ***paddle*** and let's ***skedaddle***!

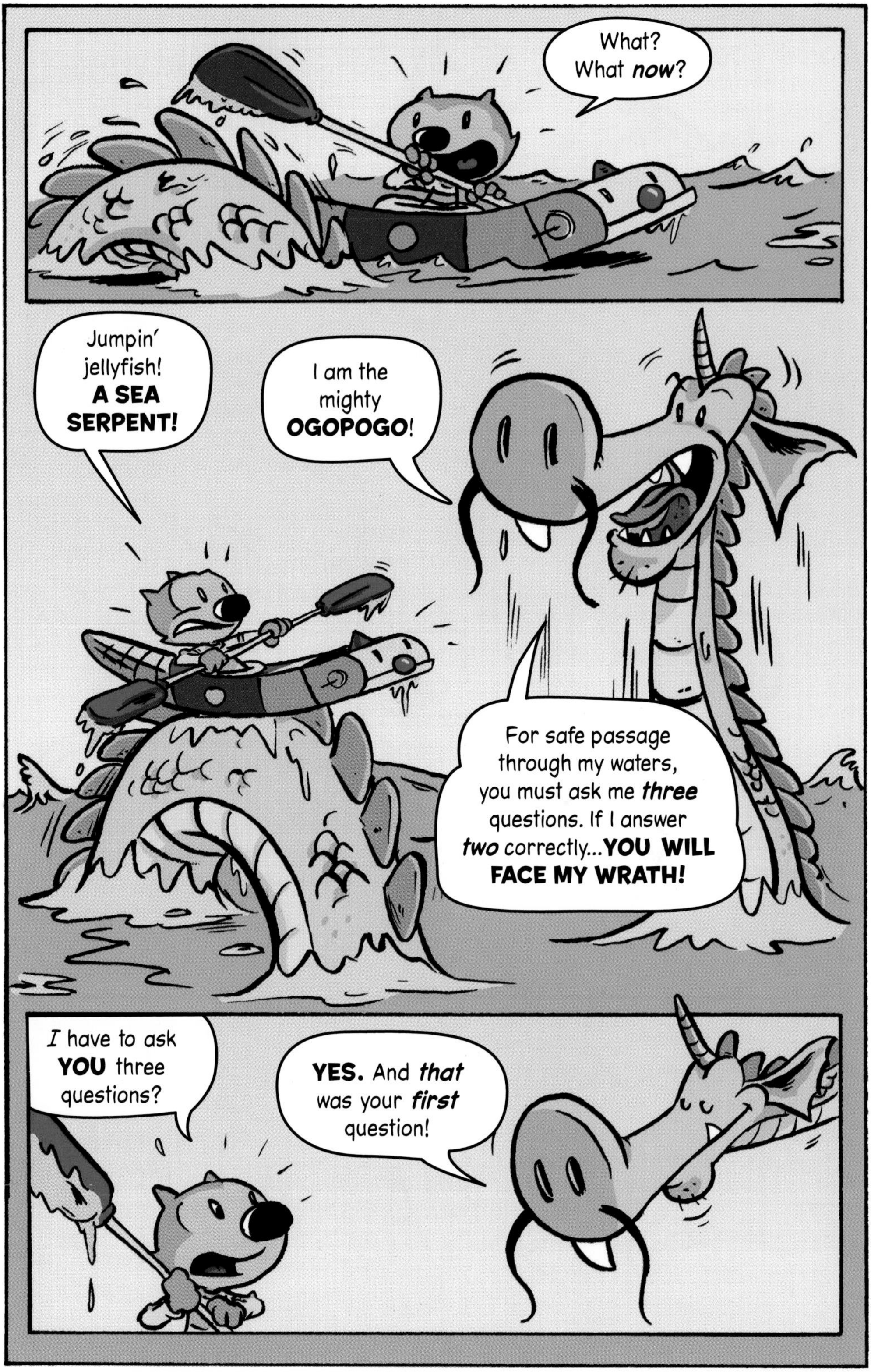
What? What *now*?
Jumpin' jellyfish! **A SEA SERPENT!**
I am the mighty **OGOPOGO**!
For safe passage through my waters, you must ask me *three* questions. If I answer *two* correctly...**YOU WILL FACE MY WRATH!**
I have to ask **YOU** three questions?
YES. And *that* was your *first* question!

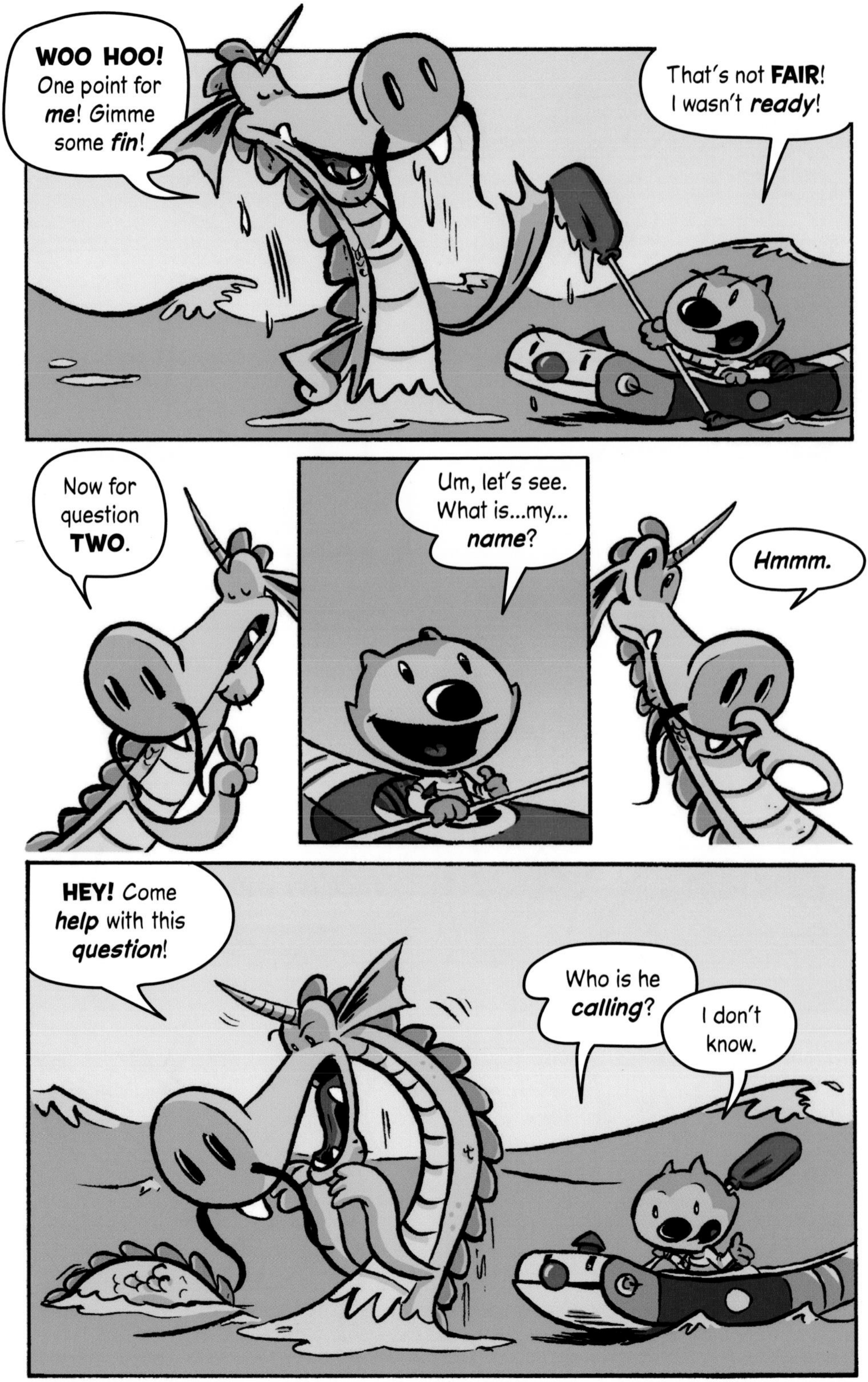
WOO HOO! One point for me! Gimme some fin!
That's not FAIR! I wasn't ready!
Now for question TWO.
Um, let's see. What is...my... name?
Hmmm.
HEY! Come help with this question!
Who is he calling?
I don't know.

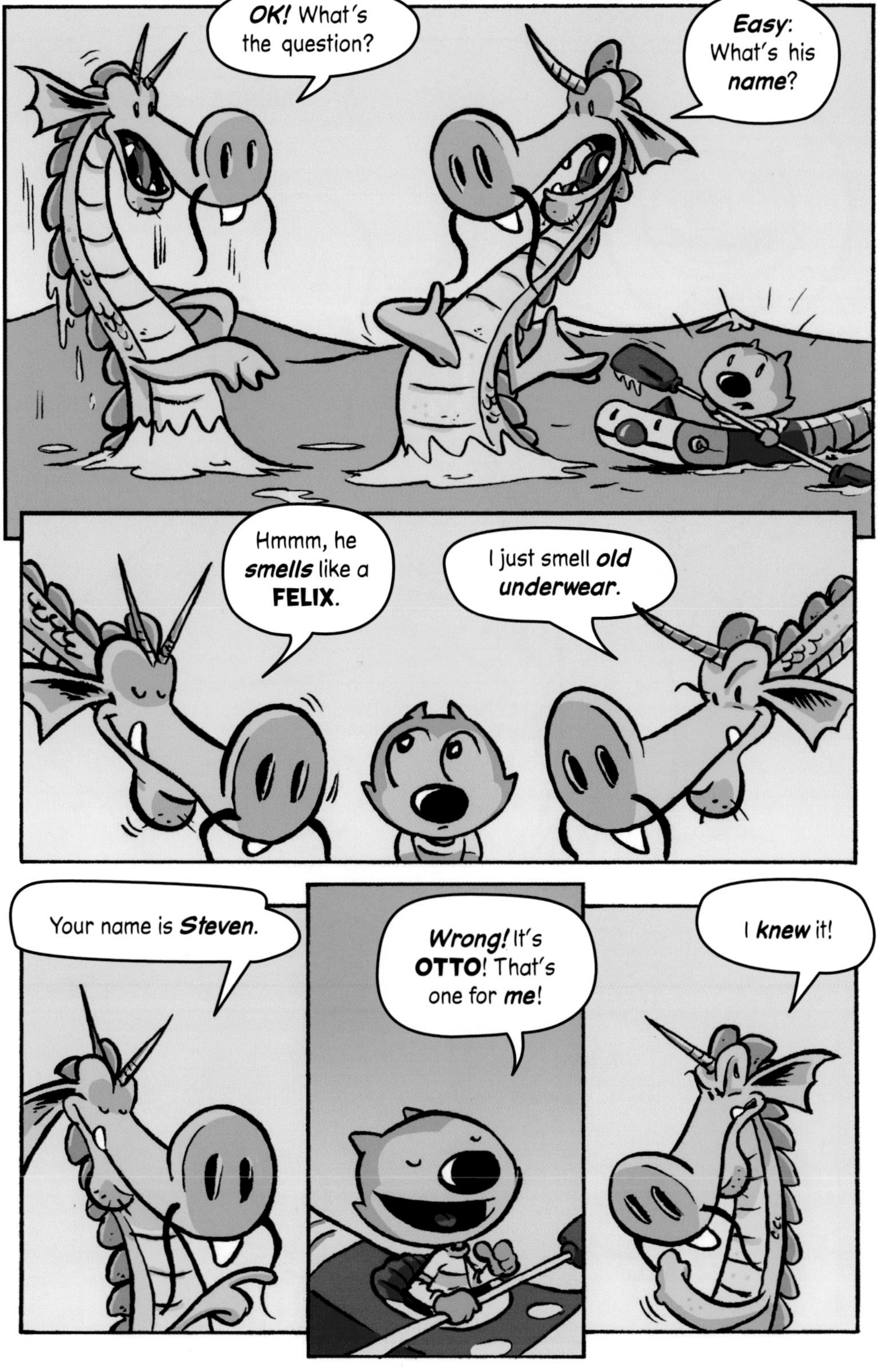
OK! What's the question?
Easy: What's his name?
Hmmm, he smells like a FELIX.
I just smell old underwear.
Your name is Steven.
Wrong! It's OTTO! That's one for me!
I knew it!

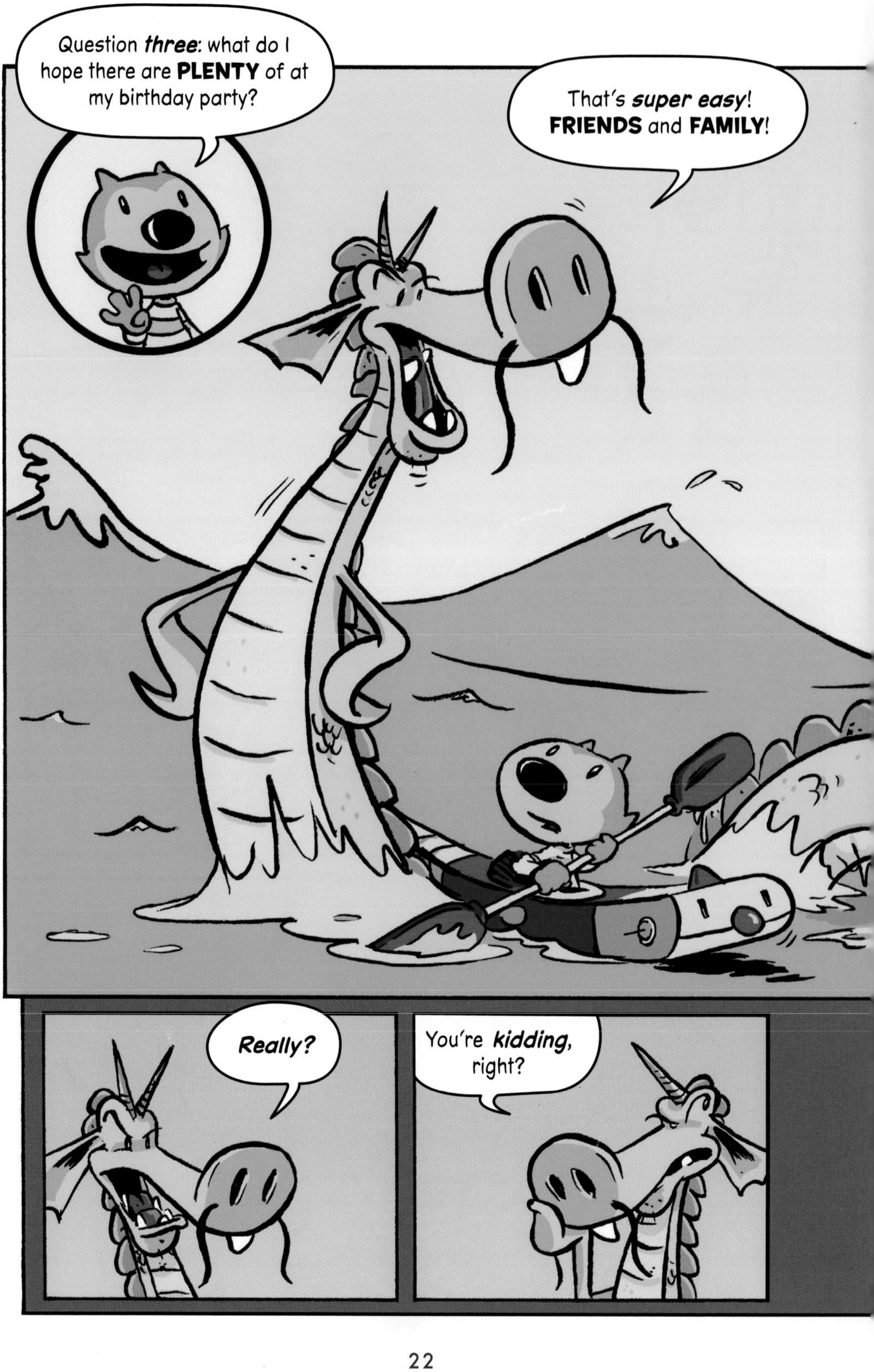
Question *three*: what do I hope there are **PLENTY** of at my birthday party?
That's ***super easy***! **FRIENDS** and **FAMILY**!
Really?
You're ***kidding***, right?

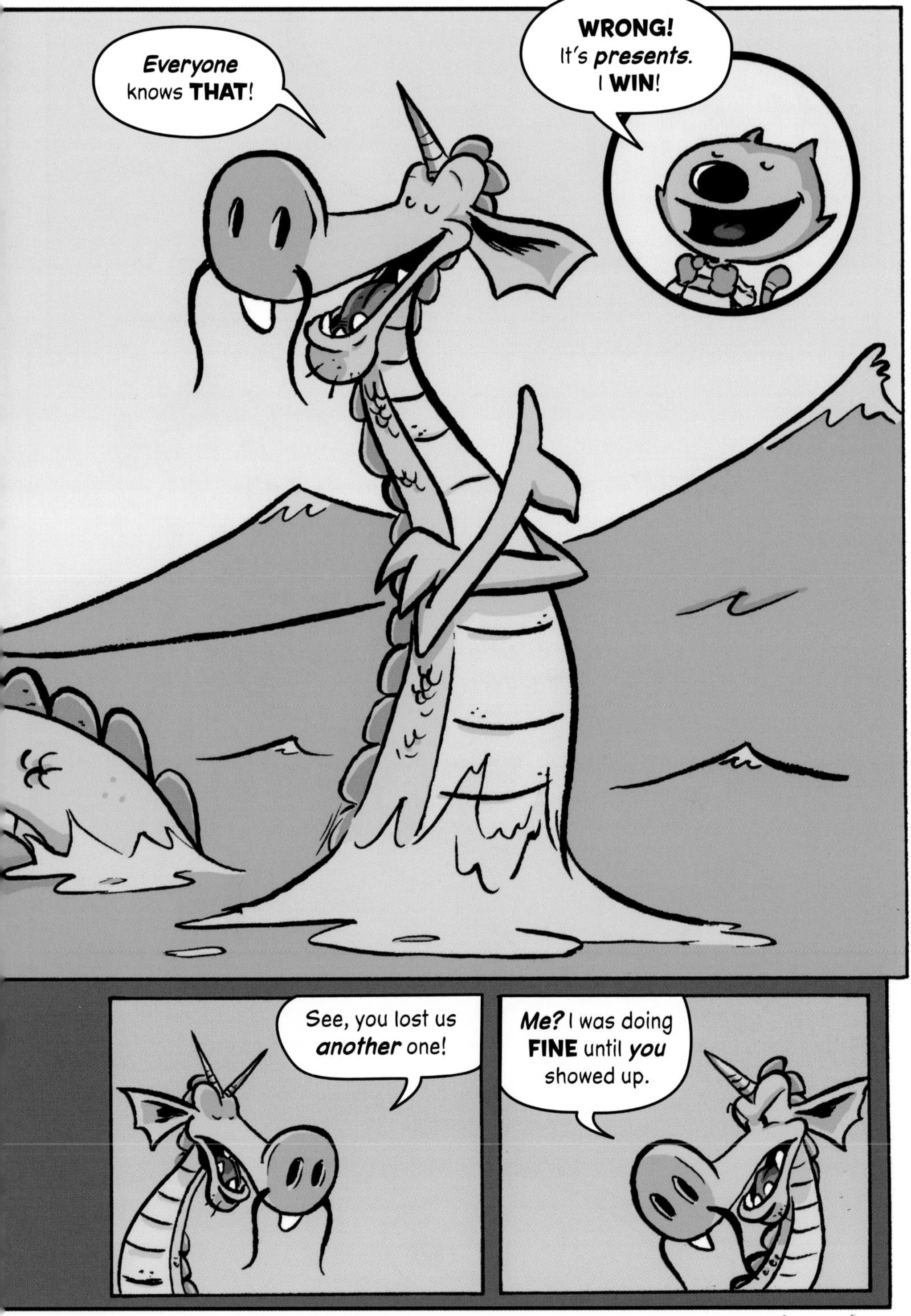
Everyone knows **THAT**!
WRONG! It's *presents.* I **WIN**!
See, you lost us *another* one!
Me? I was doing **FINE** until *you* showed up.

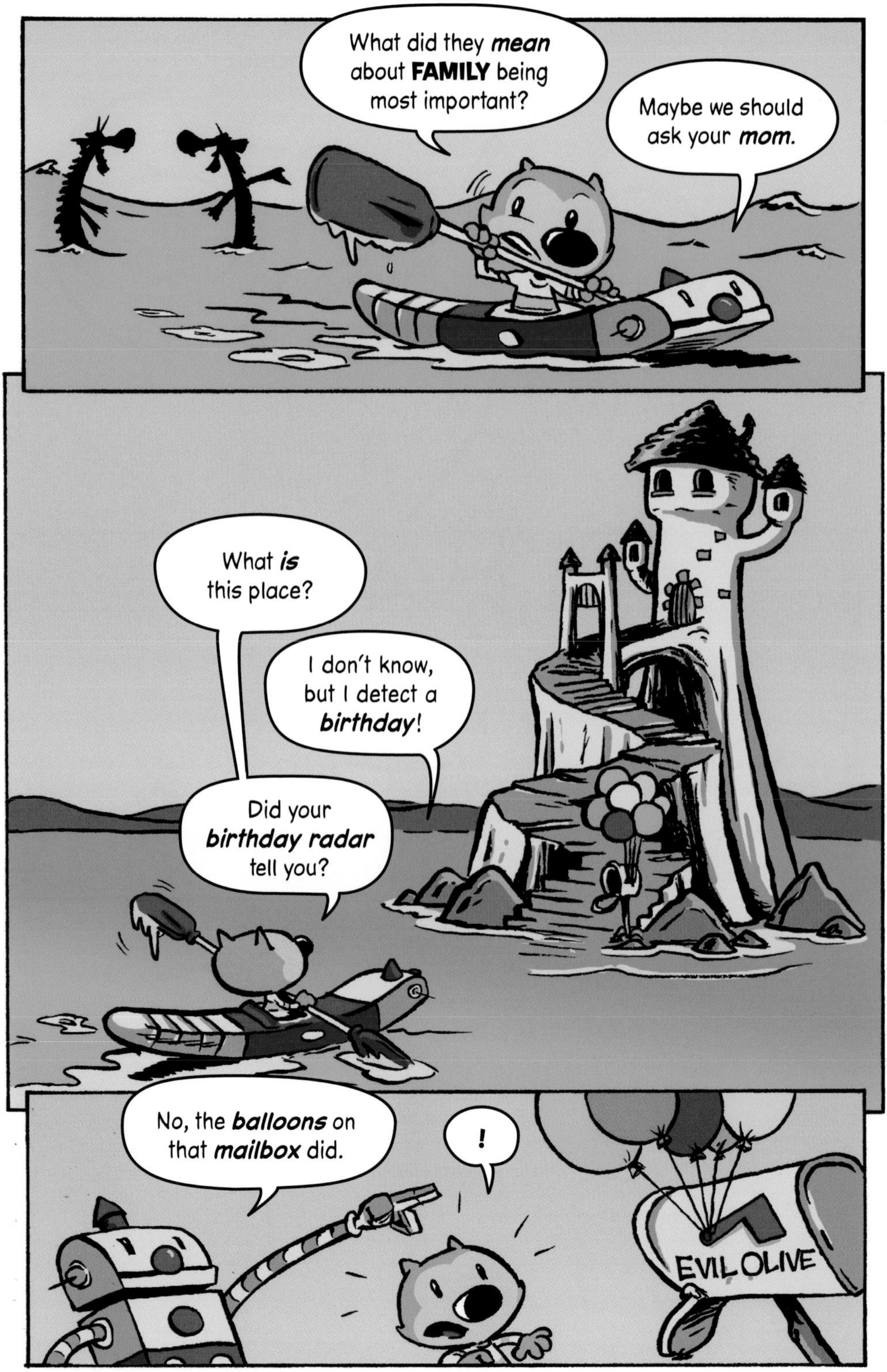
What did they *mean* about **FAMILY** being most important?
Maybe we should ask your *mom.*
What *is* this place?
I don't know, but I detect a *birthday*!
Did your *birthday radar* tell you?
No, the *balloons* on that *mailbox* did.
!
EVIL OLIVE

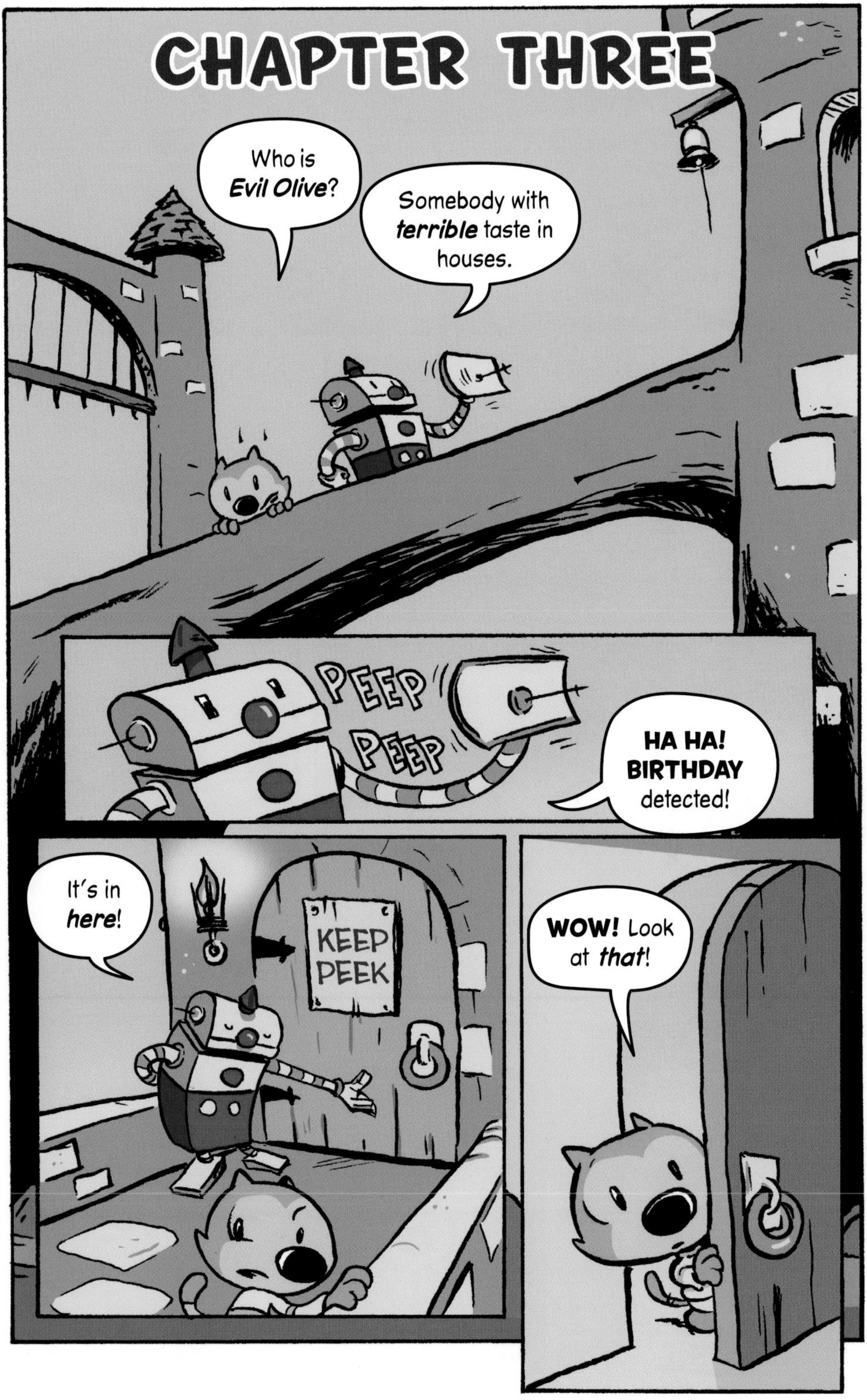
CHAPTER THREE
Who is *Evil Olive*?
Somebody with *terrible* taste in houses.
PEEP PEEP
HA HA! BIRTHDAY detected!
It's in *here*!
KEEP PEEK
WOW! Look at *that*!

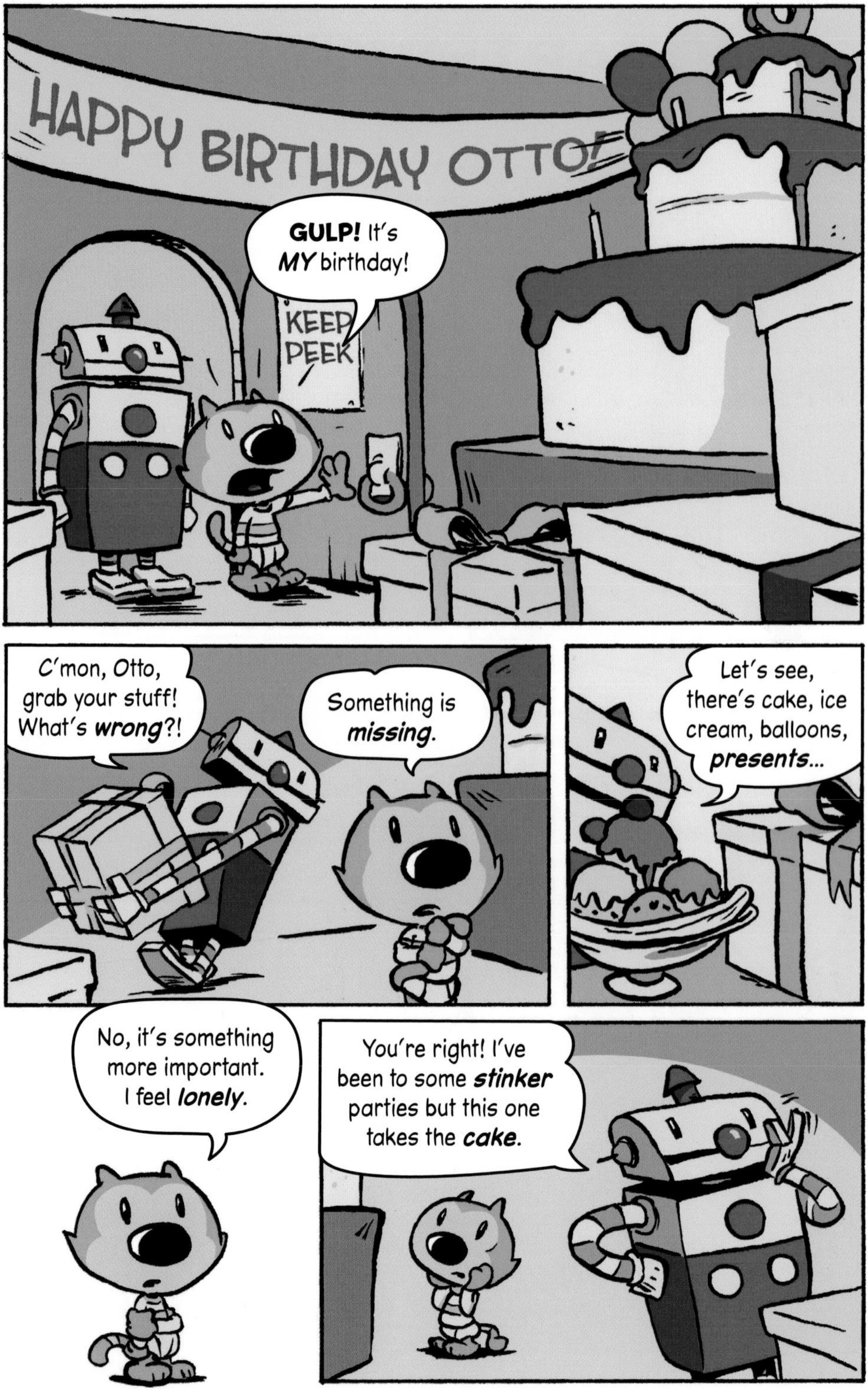
HAPPY BIRTHDAY OTTO!
GULP! It's MY birthday!
KEEP PEEK
C'mon, Otto, grab your stuff! What's wrong?!
Something is missing.
Let's see, there's cake, ice cream, balloons, presents...
No, it's something more important. I feel lonely.
You're right! I've been to some stinker parties but this one takes the cake.

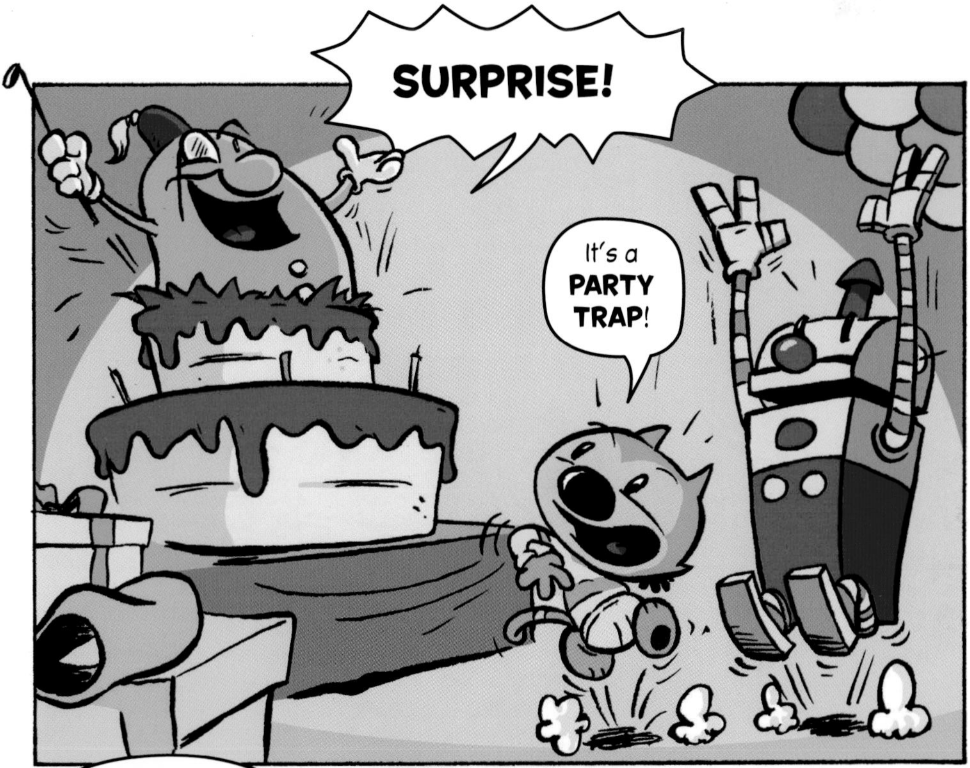
SURPRISE!
It's a PARTY TRAP!

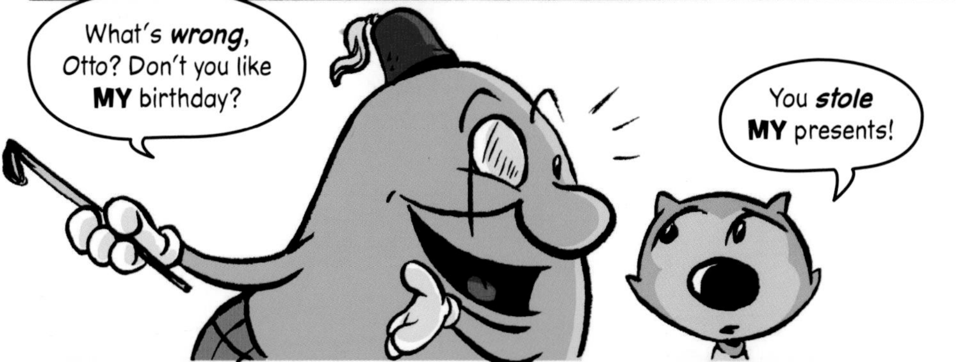
What's *wrong*, Otto? Don't you like **MY** birthday?
You *stole* **MY** presents!

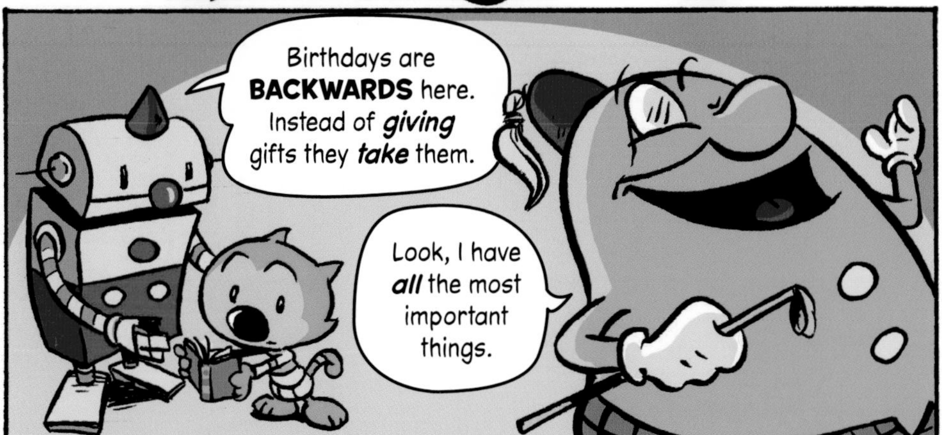
Birthdays are **BACKWARDS** here. Instead of *giving* gifts they *take* them.
Look, I have *all* the most important things.

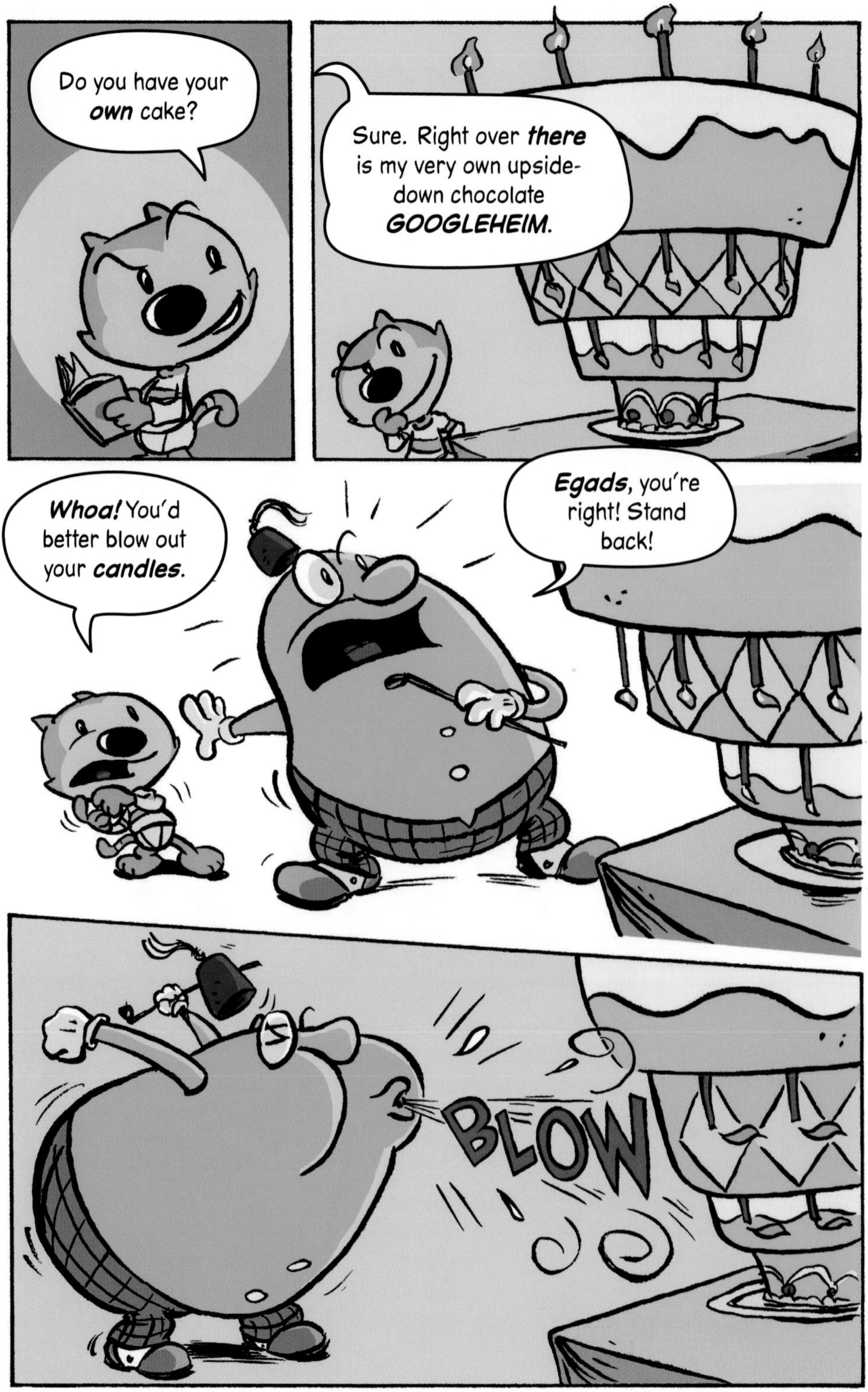
Do you have your *own* cake?
Sure. Right over *there* is my very own upside-down chocolate ***GOOGLEHEIM***.
Whoa! You'd better blow out your ***candles***.
Egads, you're right! Stand back!
BLOW

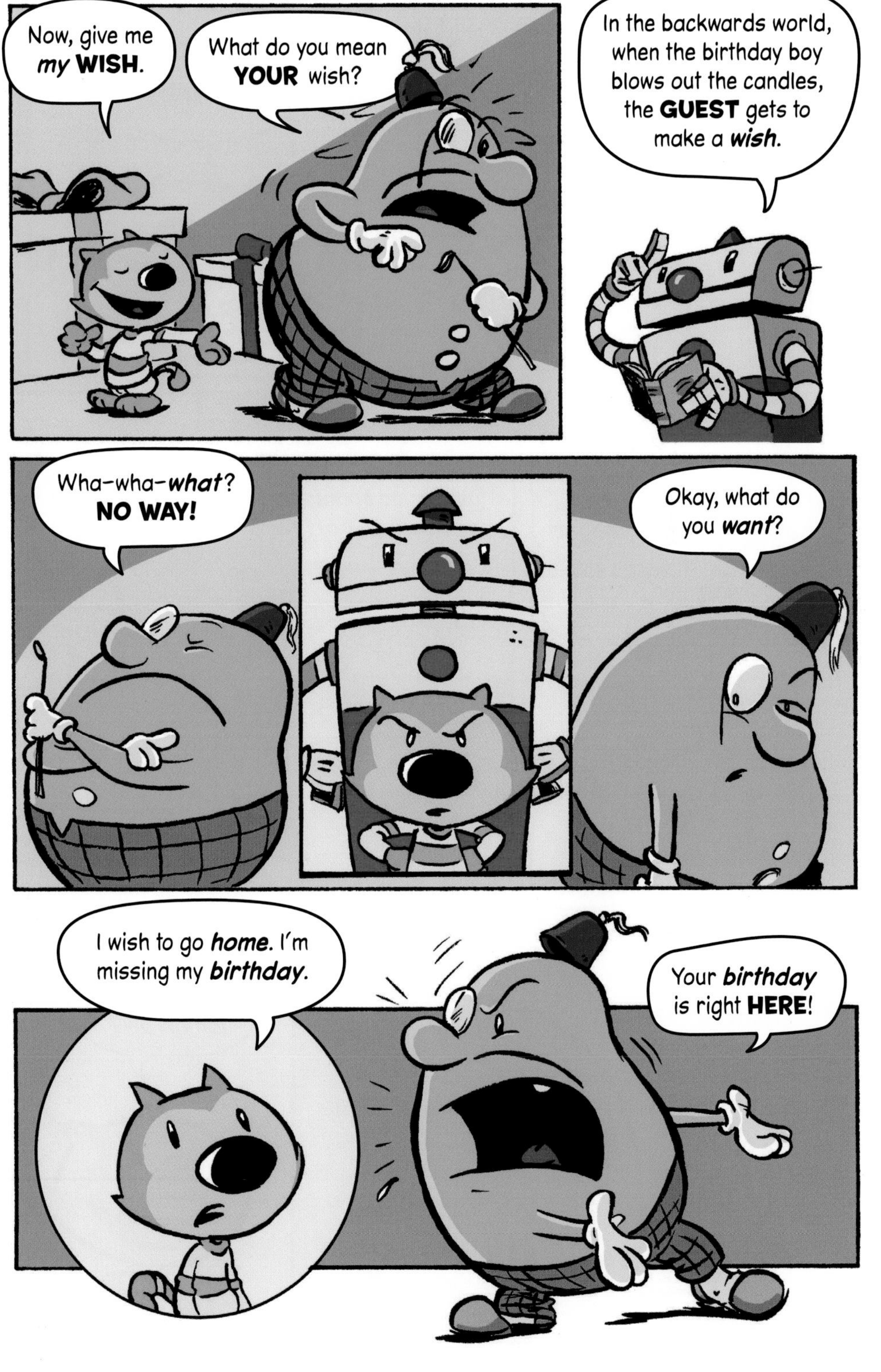

Now, give me *my* **WISH**.
What do you mean **YOUR** wish?
In the backwards world, when the birthday boy blows out the candles, the **GUEST** gets to make a ***wish***.
Wha-wha-***what***? **NO WAY!**
Okay, what do you ***want***?
I wish to go ***home***. I'm missing my ***birthday***.
Your ***birthday*** is right **HERE**!

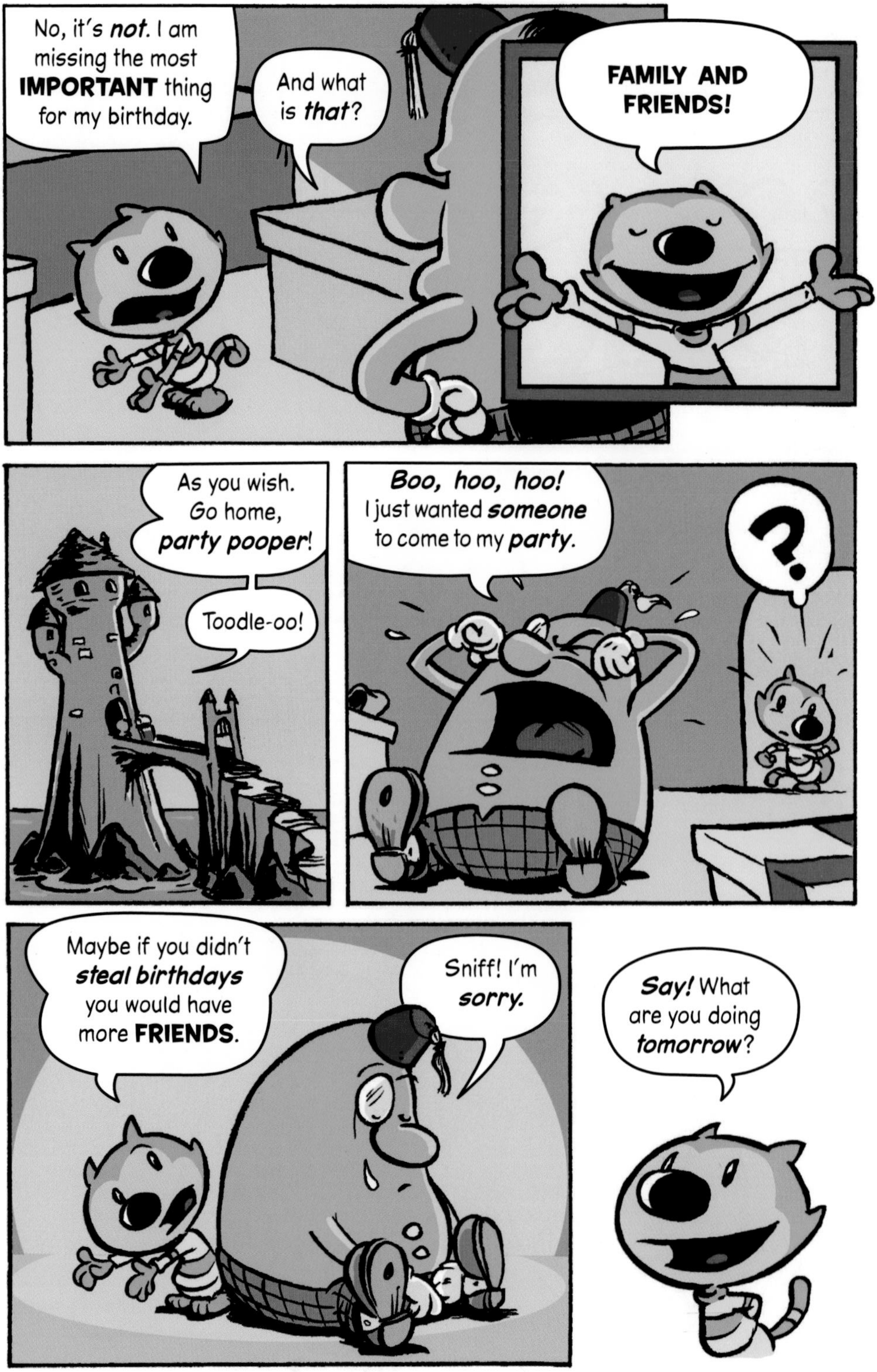

No, it's ***not.*** I am missing the most **IMPORTANT** thing for my birthday.
And what is ***that***?
FAMILY AND FRIENDS!
As you wish. Go home, ***party pooper***!
Toodle-oo!
Boo, hoo, hoo! I just wanted ***someone*** to come to my ***party***.
?
Maybe if you didn't ***steal birthdays*** you would have more **FRIENDS**.
Sniff! I'm ***sorry.***
Say! What are you doing ***tomorrow***?

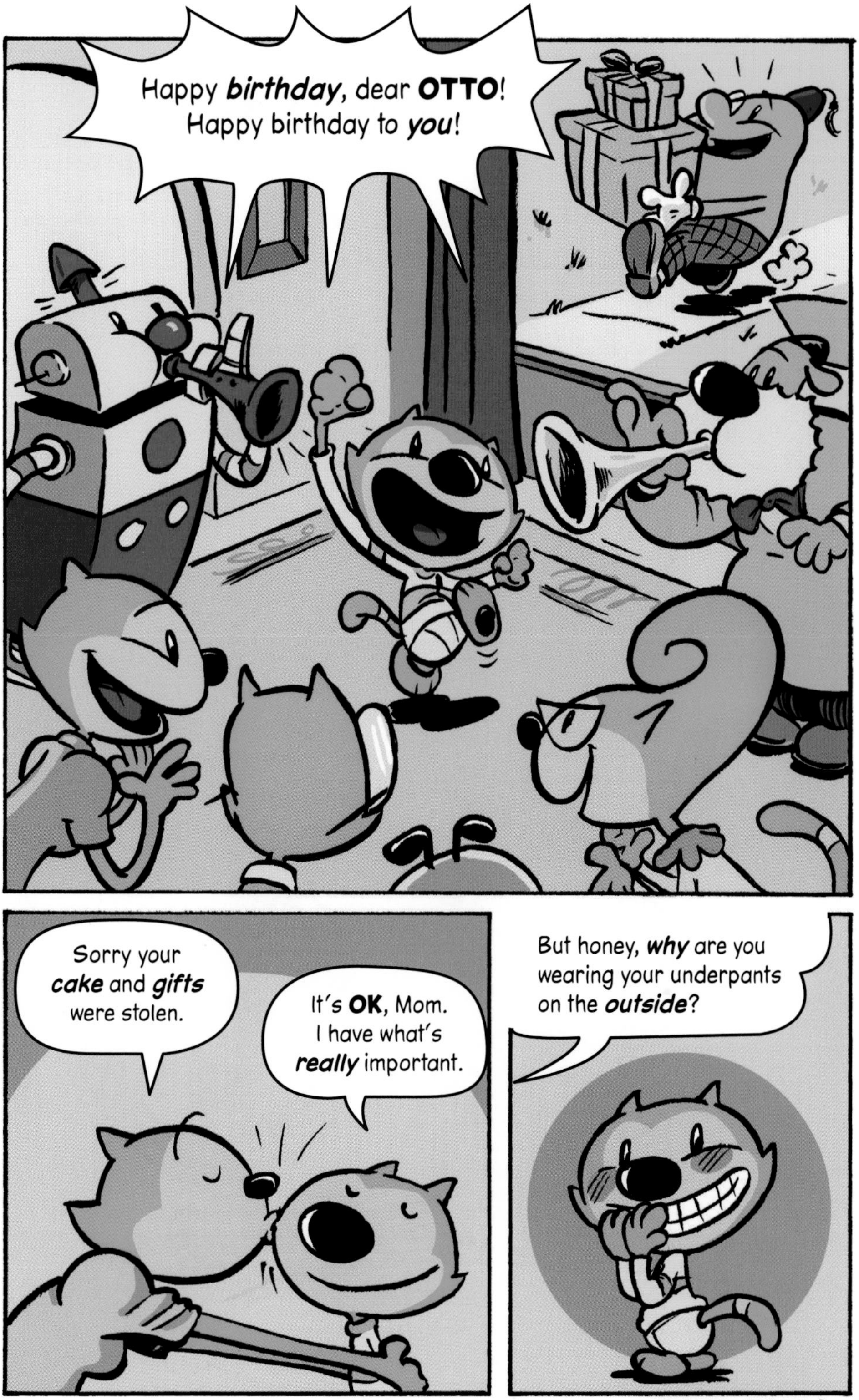
Happy birthday, dear OTTO! Happy birthday to you!
Sorry your cake and gifts were stolen.
It's OK, Mom. I have what's really important.
But honey, why are you wearing your underpants on the outside?

THE END!

ABOUT THE AUTHORS

FRANK CAMMUSO, who wrote and drew Otto's adventure, is the author of the graphic novel series *Knights of the Lunch Table*, a middle school version of King Arthur and his knights. His forthcoming series is *The Misadventures of Salem Hyde*. His writing has appeared in *The New Yorker*, *The New York Times*, *The Village Voice*, and *Slate*. **JAY LYNCH**, also a cartoonist, has helped create some of Topps Chewing Gum's most popular humor products, such as *Wacky Packages* and *Garbage Pail Kids*. Frank and Jay collaborated on the original TOON Book, *Otto's Orange Day*, which *School Library Journal* named a "Best New Book" and described as "a page-turner that beginning readers will likely wear out from dangerously high levels of enjoyment."

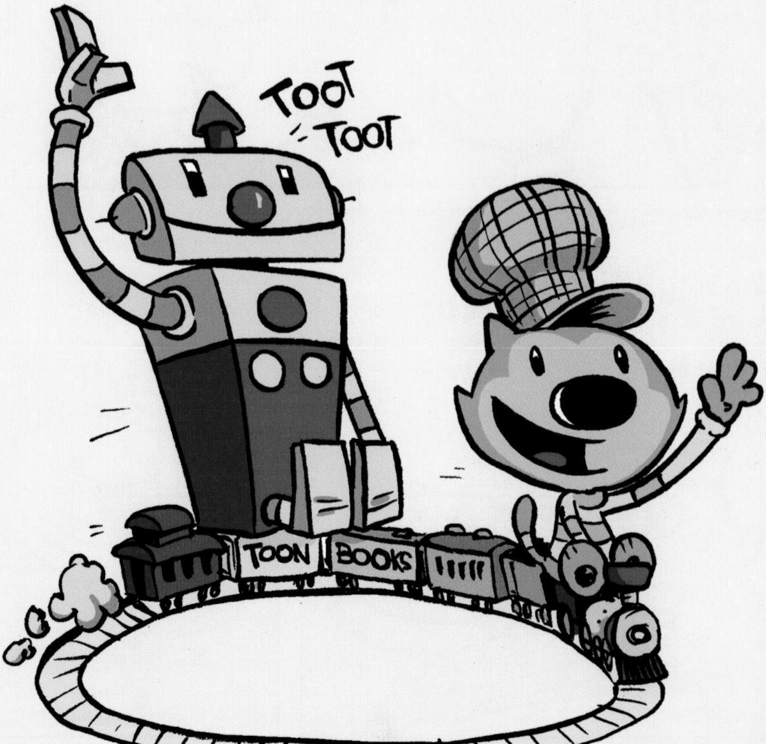
TOOT
TOOT
TOON
BOOKS

TIPS FOR PARENTS AND TEACHERS:
HOW TO READ COMICS WITH KIDS

Kids **love** comics! They are naturally drawn to the details in the pictures, which make them want to read the words. Comics beg for repeated readings and let both emerging and reluctant readers enjoy complex stories with a rich vocabulary. But since comics have their own grammar, here are a few tips for reading them with kids:

GUIDE YOUNG READERS: Use your finger to show your place in the text, but keep it at the bottom of the speaking character so it doesn't hide the very important facial expressions.

HAM IT UP! Think of the comic book story as a play and don't hesitate to read with expression and intonation. Assign parts or get kids to supply the sound effects, a great way to reinforce phonics skills.

LET THEM GUESS. Comics provide lots of context for the words, so emerging readers can make informed guesses. Like jigsaw puzzles, comics ask readers to make connections, so check a young audience's understanding by asking "What's this character thinking?" (but don't be surprised if a kid finds some of the comics' subtle details faster than you).

TALK ABOUT THE PICTURES. Point out how the artist paces the story with pauses (silent panels) or speeded-up action (a burst of short panels). Discuss how the size and shape of the panels carry meaning.

ABOVE ALL, ENJOY! There is of course never one right way to read, so go for the shared pleasure. Once children make the story happen in their imaginations, they have discovered the thrill of reading, and you won't be able to stop them. At that point, just go get them more books, and more comics.

www.TOON-BOOKS.com

SEE OUR FREE ONLINE CARTOON MAKERS, LESSON PLANS, AND MUCH MORE

TOON INTO READING!™

LEVEL 1

GRADES K–1

LEXILE BR–100 • GUIDED READING E–J • READING RECOVERY 7–12

FIRST COMICS FOR BRAND-NEW READERS

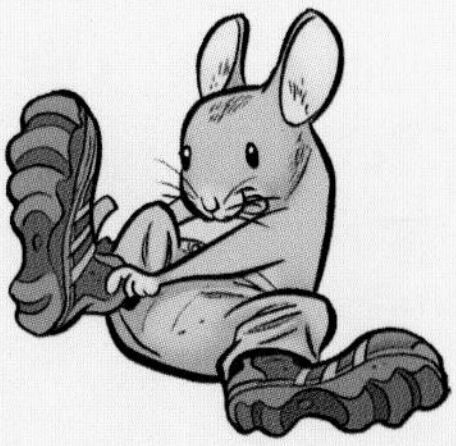

- 200–300 easy sight words
- short sentences
- often one character
- single time frame or theme
- 1–2 panels per page

LEVEL 2

GRADES 1–2

LEXILE BR–240 • GUIDED READING G–K • READING RECOVERY 11–18

EASY-TO-READ COMICS FOR EMERGING READERS

- 300–700 words
- short sentences and repetition
- story arc with few characters in a small world
- 1–4 panels per page

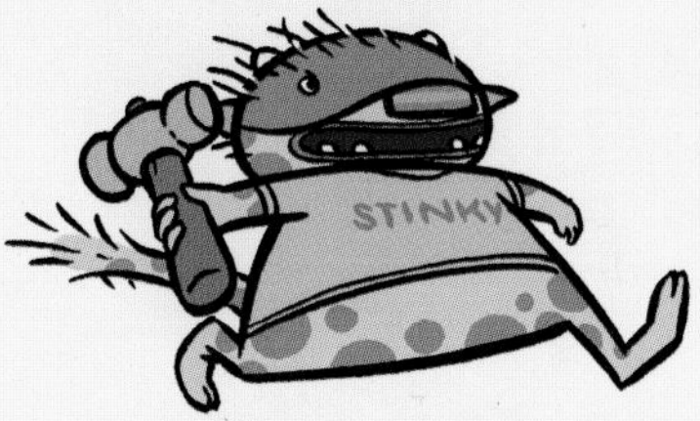
STINKY

LEVEL 3

GRADES 2–3

LEXILE 150–300 • GUIDED READING K–P • READING RECOVERY 18–20

CHAPTER-BOOK COMICS FOR ADVANCED BEGINNERS

- 800–1000+ words in long sentences
- broad world as well as shifts in time and place
- long story divided in chapters
- reader needs to make connections and speculate

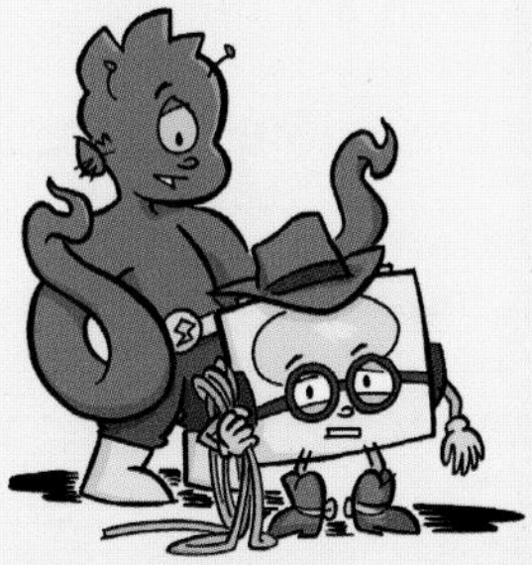

COLLECT THEM ALL!

LEVEL 1 FIRST COMICS FOR BRAND-NEW READERS

A Trip to the Bottom of the World with Mouse
Little Mouse Gets Ready
THAT'S ME!
A Toon Book by Jeff Smith
Chick & Chickie Play All Day!
What do you want to play?
I have a great idea...
A Toon Book by Claude Ponti

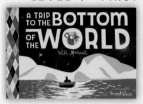

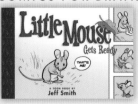

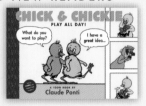

LEVEL 2 EASY-TO-READ COMICS FOR EMERGING READERS

Benny and Penny in Lights Out!
Benny, where are you GOING?
Geoffrey Hayes
Benjamin Bear
Bright Ideas!
Philippe Coudray
The big wet balloon
Liniers
Luke on the Loose
WHERE could those pigeons be hiding?
A Toon Book by Harry Bliss
Maya makes a Mess
Rutu Modan

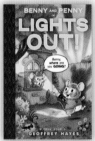

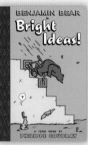

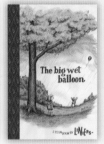

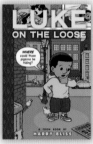

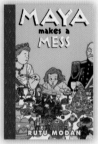

LEVEL 3 CHAPTER-BOOK COMICS FOR ADVANCED BEGINNERS

Otto's Backwards Day
A Toon Book by Frank Cammuso
The Shark King
R. Kikuo Johnson
The Cow
Otto's Orange Day
I wish that EVERYTHING was orange!
A Toon Book by Jay Lynch & Frank Cammuso
Mo and Jo
Fighting Together Forever
Jay Lynch & Dean Haspiel

TOON BOOKS

Set 1 • 10 hardcover books	**978-1-61479-147-8**
Benny and Penny in Just Pretend	978-1-61479-148-5
Benny and Penny in the Toy Breaker	978-1-61479-149-2
Chick & Chickie Play All Day!	978-1-61479-150-8
Jack and the Box	978-1-61479-151-5
Mo and Jo Fighting Together Forever	978-1-61479-152-2
Nina in That Makes Me Mad!	978-1-61479-153-9
Otto's Orange Day	978-1-61479-154-6
Silly Lilly and the Four Seasons	978-1-61479-155-3
Silly Lilly in What Will I Be Today?	978-1-61479-156-0
Zig and Wikki in Something Ate My Homework	978-1-61479-157-7

Set 2 • 8 hardcover books	**978-1-61479-298-7**
Benjamin Bear in Fuzzy Thinking	978-1-61479-299-4
Benny and Penny in the Big No-No!	978-1-61479-300-7
Little Mouse Gets Ready	978-1-61479-301-4
Luke on the Loose	978-1-61479-302-1
Maya Makes a Mess	978-1-61479-303-8
Patrick in a Teddy Bear's Picnic and Other Stories	978-1-61479-304-5
The Shark King	978-1-61479-305-2
Zig and Wikki in the Cow	978-1-61479-306-9

Set 3 • 6 hardcover books	**978-1-61479-422-6**
Benjamin Bear in Bright Ideas!	978-1-61479-423-3
Benny and Penny in Lights Out!	978-1-61479-424-0
The Big Wet Balloon	978-1-61479-425-7
Otto's Backwards Day	978-1-61479-426-4
Patrick Eats His Peas and Other Stories	978-1-61479-427-1
A Trip to the Bottom of the World with Mouse	978-1-61479-428-8

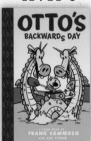

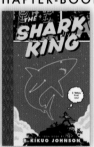

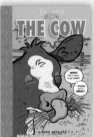

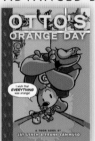

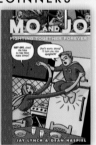